LUNCH MONEY

Andrew Clements

Illustrations by Brian Selznick

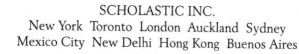

SCHOLASTIC INC.
New York Toronto London Auckland Sydney
Mexico City New Delhi Hong Kong Buenos Aires

For my dad, Bill Clements

No part of this publication may be reproduced, stored in a retrieval system, or transmitted in any form or by any means, electronic, mechanical, photocopying, recording, or otherwise, without written permission of the publisher. For information regarding permission, write to Simon & Schuster Books for Young Readers, Simon & Schuster Children's Publishing Division, 1230 Avenue of the Americas, New York, NY 10020.

ISBN 0-439-85088-6

12 11 10 9 8 7 6 5 4 3 2 1   6 7 8 9 10 11/0

Printed in the U.S.A.   23

First Scholastic printing, January 2006

The text for this book is set in Revival.
The illustrations for this book are rendered in pencil.

Book design by Greg Stadnyk

Chapter 1

TALENT

Greg Kenton had heaps of talent. He was good at baseball, and even better at soccer. He had a clear singing voice, and he also played the piano. He was a whiz at sketching and drawing, and he did well at school—reading, science, music, writing, art, math, gym, social studies— the whole deal. But as good as he was at all these things, Greg's greatest talent had always been money.

Greg had never taken money lessons. He hadn't had a money tutor or gone to money camp. His talent with money was natural. He had always understood money. He knew how to save it, how to keep track of it, how to grow it, and most of all, how to make it.

It takes some kids years and years to figure out that everything is worth something. Not Greg. Sitting in a grocery cart by the door of the supermarket, he had watched with sharp brown eyes as his mom dropped a small metal disk into a red machine. Then she'd turned the crank, and a handful of M&M's had rattled out into her hand. Greg loved the sweet, crunchy taste, but it wasn't the candy that had captured his imagination. It was that shiny silver coin.

While he was still a skinny preschooler with curly brown hair, Greg had learned to keep his eyes and ears open. One day at breakfast his biggest brother, Ross, griped, "How come I have to make my bed? I'm just going to mess it up again tonight."

His other big brother, Edward, chimed in, "And cleaning up our rooms every single morning? That's not fair. Besides, they're *our* rooms."

His mom had answered, "Yes, but your rooms are in *my* house, and I like my house tidy. So if you want to keep getting your allowances every Friday, get back upstairs and fix the mess."

Ross and Edward had grumbled all the way back to their rooms. Their little brother followed them, and two minutes later Greg had started a housekeeping business: making a bed,

ten cents; putting dirty clothes in the laundry, five cents; putting clean clothes away, two cents; and hanging up used towels, three cents each.

If both his big brothers were complete slobs, and they usually were, Greg earned a little more than two dollars a week—so it was certainly not a get-rich-quick scheme. But that wasn't what Greg was trying to do. He was perfectly happy to get rich slowly, because being patient is a big part of having money talent. Greg understood that a year has fifty-two weeks. So between the ages of four and six Greg transformed rumpled sheets, used underwear, smelly socks, and soggy towels into beautiful, spendable cash—more than two hundred dollars. Then his mom shut down his business, insisting that Ross and Edward had to do their own chores.

When he was still in nursery school, Greg had taken charge of recycling the family's trash. He emptied all the waste baskets at least once a week. At the bins out in the garage, he sorted the newspapers and magazines from the cardboard, the aluminum from the steel, and the ♳ plastic from the ♴ plastic. As a reward for this service, which took him only ten minutes a week, Greg was allowed to keep the deposit refunds on all the cans and bottles. This added up to about four dollars a month in the cool seasons and eight dollars a month during the long, thirsty summer.

As a seven and eight-year-old, Greg had found other ways to make money around the house and yard. He shined his dad's and mom's dress shoes for fifty cents a pair. He scrubbed black heel marks and old wax off the floor tiles in the kitchen for ten cents a square. He dug dandelions out of the lawn at the rate of four for a nickel. And he picked Japanese beetles off the shrubs for a penny a bug.

At first Greg enjoyed simply *having* the

money he made. Cash was fun and interesting all by itself. He liked sorting and stacking the bills—singles, fives, tens, twenties, and even a few fifties he'd gotten from his grandparents for Christmas. He studied the faces of the famous presidents, and Alexander Hamilton, too—who he discovered was never president, only the first secretary of the treasury of the United States. He looked at the engraving on the bills with a magnifying glass, studying the tiny face of Lincoln sitting there on his big square chair inside the Lincoln Memorial on the back of every five-dollar bill.

Greg found the coins just as interesting. He loved making rolls of quarters, dimes, nickels, and pennies, stacks and stacks of them. And the golden Sacagawea dollar coins? He didn't put them into rolls. He  had collected twenty-seven of them, which he kept hidden in a sock in the bottom drawer of his dresser. Every once in a while he'd spread them out on his bed and count them again.

Greg also became an amateur coin collector.

It was exciting to come up with a Mercury dime now and then, and he'd found a couple dozen of those gray pennies that had been made out of steel instead of copper during the Second World War. He had found pennies that were worth ten dollars or more, and that can get a kid thinking.

As nice as it was to have the money itself, Greg quickly learned it was also fun to spend some now and then. He would spend it for something special, like his own professional-quality soccer ball, or one of those huge aluminum flashlights with six batteries, that could throw a beam of light all the way across the lake at his grampa's cabin. He bought cool stuff that he really wanted, and mostly when it seemed too long a wait until his birthday or Christmas. He bought collectible baseball cards, and he had also bought a few Beanie Babies and then sold them for a nice profit. Sometimes he bought comic books, but only a few, and only ones that looked like they would become more valuable. Greg loved comics, but he got to read all he wanted for free because his dad collected them.

By the time he got to third grade, Greg had

set himself a goal. He wanted to be rich. He thought it would be fantastic to be able to spend all the money he wanted, anytime he felt like it. If he wanted to get the world's fastest computer plus a hundred of the best games, no problem. If he wanted a car, a speedboat, a house in the mountains, a home-theater system, or even a whole island out in the middle of the Pacific—plus his own sea-plane and a private crew to fly him there—no problem. Greg was sure that someday he'd be able to get anything he wanted. All he'd need was money.

And he wasn't that different from his friends. A lot of them also dreamed about get-ting rich, and some of them wanted to be famous, too. Greg didn't care much about fame. What was the point? Besides, he figured that if he got rich enough, really superrich, then the famous part would happen automati-cally anyway. But there was one big difference between Greg and most of his friends. He wasn't just dreaming about getting rich. He was working at it.

As Greg reached third grade and then fourth, his whole neighborhood had become the land of opportunity. He was thin, but wiry, and strong enough to tackle any job he put his mind to. Greg raked and bagged leaves in the fall and again in the spring. He washed cars all spring, summer, and fall, and on hot days he sold lemonade. He shoveled snow and salted icy sidewalks in the winter. Greg became a feeder of cats, a walker of dogs, and a collector of mail and newspapers for people on vacation. He swept garages and straightened up messy basements. If people ever decided to throw things away, Greg kept the good stuff for himself and hauled it home to his own little corner of the Kenton family garage. And when he had collected enough interesting junk, Greg would drag it all out to the end of the driveway, put up a sign, and hold a sale. Neighborhood money filled Greg's pockets the way rain fills puddles.

For example, consider what Greg earned just from shoveling snow. He had eight customers within two blocks of his house, and every time it snowed, he shoveled their front walks for a flat rate: ten dollars. The winter of his third-grade year, it snowed six times, and the winter of his fourth-grade year it snowed five times. And eleven snowfalls times eight customers equals eighty-eight shovel sessions, times ten dollars for each one equals *eight hundred and eighty dollars*—which isn't just a lot of money to a nine-year-old. Eight hundred and eighty dollars is a lot of money to anybody.

It hadn't taken Greg long to become the family banker. If his mom and dad were running late for a movie on a Saturday night, Greg was happy to lend them twenty dollars—as long as they signed his little record book and promised to repay the money. And his parents got special treatment. They didn't have to pay Greg's usual lending fees. After all, they didn't charge him for the food he ate, or for the safe, warm bed he slept in every night. So that seemed fair. But his two brothers had to pay the regular rates.

If his older brother needed an extra five dollars to get that new baseball glove in time to break it in before the Babe Ruth tryouts, Greg was happy to lend him the money—as long as Edward signed the book and promised to pay back the five dollars one week later, *plus* a fifty-cent fee—*and* Greg got the old mitt as part of the deal, because a used baseball glove might be worth something at his next driveway sale. And if Ross just *had* to have that hot new CD the instant it arrived at the music store, he knew his little brother would be happy to help—for a fee.

Both Ross and Edward made fun of Greg's moneymaking schemes. They called him Scrooge and Mr. Cashman and Old Moneybags, and some other nicknames too. Still, whenever they needed money, they knew they would always be welcome at the First Family Bank of Greg.

One Thursday shortly after Greg had finished fourth grade, his dad pulled a reference book off a shelf next to the computer in the family room. Along with the information he'd been looking for, he also found twelve five-dollar bills tucked between the pages. Only one person in the family could have owned that money, so at bedtime that night, he told Greg that he'd found it.

Greg sat straight up in bed. "You put it all back, right?"

His dad said, "Absolutely. But how about we go to the bank on Saturday morning and open up a savings account? That's where your money belongs."

Greg had looked at him suspiciously. "Why?"

"Because your money will be safe at the bank, and it'll be there when you need it. Like when you go to college."

Greg said, "But can I get my money out before then? Like if I see something I need at a yard sale?"

His dad nodded. "You're allowed to get your money anytime you want. But if you take the money out of the bank, then the money won't grow."

"'Grow'?" said Greg. "You mean 'earn interest,' right?"

A little surprised, his dad had nodded and said, "Right. Earn interest. If you put a hundred dollars in the bank and leave it there for one year, the bank will add five dollars more to it, so then you'll have a hundred and five dollars. That's called earning five percent interest a year. And all the money has to do is sit there. Pretty neat, huh?"

Greg thought about that. "So my money just sits there?"

His dad said, "Well, actually, the bank will probably lend your money to other people, and then those other people will pay the bank interest for being able to use it—just like the bank pays you that five dollars of interest so that it can use *your* money."

Greg said, "And I only get *five dollars* if I let the bank use my *hundred* dollars for a whole year? That stinks. Because if I spend two dollars on lemon juice and sugar and paper cups, and if I sell thirty cups of lemonade this weekend, then in one weekend I'll make more money than the bank would pay me all year."

"That's true," his dad said. "Making your own business investments is a way to earn more money faster—as long as you make good investments. But if you keep hiding money around the house, it could get lost. Or stolen."

"But what about your comic books?" Greg asked. "You keep your whole collection right here in the house."

His dad nodded. "True, but I've got an insurance policy on them, and a special policy on the most valuable ones. And if something happened to my comics, the insurance company would pay me back the money they're worth. But you can't get an insurance policy on money itself—unless you keep it in a bank. So if our house burned down, you'd have no money at all—none. And you'd get nothing back."

That got Greg's attention.

The next day Greg had retrieved money from about thirty different hiding places around the house and yard and garage. And on Saturday morning he'd gone to the bank and opened his own savings account with a first deposit that amazed his dad—more than three thousand two hundred dollars. And that wasn't even all of Greg's money, just most of it. He'd kept a couple hundred dollars at home, because Greg already understood that sometimes a business person needs money right away.

By age eleven he was well on his way to success, always on the lookout for new money-making opportunities. And then one day Greg Kenton made the greatest financial discovery of his young life.

Chapter 2

QUARTERS

It was near the end of his fifth-grade year. Around eleven thirty one morning during silent reading Greg felt hungry, so he had started to think about his lunch: a ham-and-cheese sandwich, a bag of nacho cheese Doritos, a bunch of red grapes, and an apple-cherry juice box.

His mom had made him a bag lunch, which was fine with Greg. Making a lunch was a lot cheaper than buying one, and Greg loved saving money whenever possible. Plus home food was usually better than school food. And on days he brought a bag lunch his mom also gave him fifty cents to buy dessert. Which was also fine with Greg. Sometimes he bought a treat, and sometimes he held on to the money. On this particular day he had been planning to spend both quarters on an ice-cream sandwich.

Then Greg remembered where his lunch

was: at home on the kitchen counter. He did have a dollar of his own money in his wallet, and he had two quarters from his mom in his front pocket, but a whole school lunch cost two bucks. He needed two more quarters.

So Greg had walked to the front of the classroom, waited until his teacher looked up from her book, and then said, "Mrs. McCormick, I left my lunch at home. May I borrow fifty cents?"

Mrs. McCormick had not missed a teaching opportunity in over twenty years. So she shook her head, and in a voice loud enough for the whole class to hear, she said, "I'm sorry, but no, I will not lend you money. Do you know what would happen if I handed out fifty cents to all the boys and girls who forgot their lunches? I'd go broke, that's what. You need to learn to remember these things for yourself."

Then, turning to the class, Mrs. McCormick had announced, "Greg needs some lunch money. Can someone lend him fifty cents?"

Over half of the kids in the class raised a hand.

Embarrassed, Greg had hurried over to

Brian Lemont, and Brian handed him two quarters.

"Thanks," Greg said. "Pay you back tomorrow."

Ten minutes later Greg was in the cafeteria line, shaking all four quarters around in his pocket. They made a nice clinking sound, and that had reminded Greg how much he liked quarters. Stack up four, and you've got a dollar. Stack up twenty quarters, and that's five dollars. Greg remembered one day when he had piled up all his quarters on his dresser—four stacks, and each had been over a foot tall. Stacking up quarters like that always made Greg feel rich.

So on that day in April of his fifth-grade year, Greg had started looking around the cafeteria, and everywhere he looked, he saw quarters. He saw kids trading quarters for ice-cream sandwiches and cupcakes and cookies at the dessert table. He saw kids over at the school store trading quarters for neon pens and sparkly pencils, and for little decorations like rubber soccer balls and plastic butterflies to stick onto the ends of those new pencils. He saw Albert Hobart drop three quarters into a machine so he could have a cold can of juice with his lunch. Kids were buying extra food, fancy pens and pencils, special drinks and snacks. There were quarters all over the place, *buckets* of them.

And then Greg remembered those hands that had been raised back in his classroom, all those kids who'd had a couple of quarters to lend him—*extra* quarters.

Excited, Greg had started making some calculations in his head—another one his talents. There were about 450 fourth, fifth, and sixth graders at Ashworth Intermediate School. If even *half* of those kids had two extra quarters to spend every day, then there had to be at least *four hundred* quarters floating around the school. That was a hundred dollars a day, over *five hundred dollars* each week—money, *extra* money, just jingling around in pockets and lunch bags!

At that moment Greg's view of school changed completely and forever. School had suddenly become the most interesting place on the planet. Because young Greg Kenton had decided that school would be an excellent place to make his fortune.

Chapter 3

THE PERFECT HAMMER

The very next day Greg had started selling candy and gum in the shadow of the sliding board during lunch recess—gum was ten cents a stick, and he sold tropical fruit Starbursts at three for a quarter.

Sales were brisk, and Greg was making some money. But it was risky. Kids took the candy and gum into their classrooms, which was against school rules. And if one kid had turned him in, Greg would have found himself having a little chat with the principal, Mrs. Davenport.

So Greg began to look around for other things he could sell. He thought about the ads on TV when he watched his favorite shows. What did they always try to sell to kids—besides candy and breakfast cereals? Simple: toys.

Greg did some research on the Internet and quickly discovered dozens of companies that sold toys and souvenirs and gadgets at incredibly low prices.

"You need to do *what?*"

That's what Greg's mom had said when he told her he needed to borrow her credit card.

And Greg had explained: "I need to buy some toys—not for me. They're to sell to other kids. To make some money. This company has great stuff, and it's real cheap, but I need to order with a credit card. I can pay you back with cash right away, if that's what you're worried about."

His mom was actually worried about something else. She thought Greg spent too much time thinking about making money. Just a few days before, she had asked her husband, "Is it something we've done, to make Greg like this? All he ever thinks about is getting rich. I want him to just enjoy being a kid, hang out with his friends more, have more fun." But her husband had told her, "As far as I can see, Greg's definitely a kid. He likes to read and draw, he plays sports, and he gets good grades. I'd say he's pretty well balanced. And he seems to be having plenty of fun. This money thing is probably just a phase. Besides, there's nothing wrong with wanting to make money. Or working hard. If that's what you call a problem, then I wish some other people in this family had it too!"

So his mom had used her credit card to help Greg place an order with the Nic-Nac Novelty Company. He ordered 144 miniature troll dolls, tiny plastic creatures with big eyes and long, bright hair—blue, red, orange, and green. Then Greg paid his mom $12.00 in cash to cover the cost of the credit-card order—$10.50 for the trolls, and $1.50 for the shipping costs.

The little trolls were a huge hit at school, an instant fad. Greg sold all 144 of them in three days for a quarter each, taking in a total of thirty-six dollars—and twenty-four dollars of that money was pure profit.

But Greg didn't call it profit. He liked to think of it as "new money." Greg had taken twelve dollars he already had—that was the old money—and he had used his old money to buy 144 trolls for about eight cents apiece. Then he'd sold each one for twenty-five cents. So he had made back all twelve dollars of his old money, plus twenty-four dollars of new money.

And what did Greg do with his new money? He used it to place another, bigger order with the NicNac Novelty Company: 48 more trolls, 48 miniature superballs, 24 small jack-and-ball sets, 48 sticky-stretchy spiders, and 36 plastic rings—12 for boys and 24 for girls.

But the new items hadn't sold so well. After two weeks only about two thirds of the second order was gone. Kids had started to get bored with his products, and so had Greg. And there was another problem.

During third-period language arts one morning, he'd been called to the school office. And then he'd been shown into the principal's office.

The first thing Greg noticed was the toys on her desk. Mrs. Davenport followed his eyes and nodded at the four mini-superballs and the wad of sticky-stretchy spiders. She said, "I got the superballs from Ms. Kensing. She caught Eddie Connors and Hector Vega bouncing them up and hitting the lights on the ceiling of the gym. And I got the spiders from Mr. Percy, the custodian. He says these things have left oily marks on almost every window in the school. And Mr. Percy tells me that all the kids he asked said they bought them from you. Is that true?"

Greg nodded.

"Why are you selling toys at school?" she asked.

Greg shrugged. "To make some money. And because they're fun."

Mrs. Davenport said, "Those tiny trolls I saw all over the school a few weeks ago—were you the one selling those, too?"

Greg nodded.

The principal said, "Well, I admire your initiative, but starting right now, you may not sell any more toys at school. The boys and girls already bring plenty of other nuisance items to school, and they do *not* need extra help from you. Is that clear?"

Greg nodded and said, "Yes."

"Very well. You may return to your class now. Ask Mrs. Ogden for a pass."

Walking back to language arts that day, Greg

hadn't been discouraged. He wasn't even unhappy. He faced the fact that his novelty toy business had been doomed from the start. For one thing, kids usually get tired of toys quickly. And Greg also realized it was amazing that his toy sales hadn't been shut down even sooner. If you sell toys to kids at school, that's where the kids will play with them. And toys and school are a bad mix. Still, even though he hadn't sold all the toys from the second order, he'd made a small profit.

Greg carefully reviewed what the principal had said to him. And again, he saw the bright side. Because Mrs. Davenport had not said that he had to stop selling things at school. She had just said he had to stop selling *toys*.

So all he needed was something *else* he could sell at school, something that wouldn't upset the teachers or Mrs. Davenport. Or the custodian. Even better, it would be great to sell something they would actually approve of. But what? What?

The answer came to Greg as the first few days of summer began turning fifth grade into a fading memory. The answer was so simple, and it seemed absolutely foolproof. It would take some hard work if he wanted to have everything ready in September for the start of sixth grade, but hard work was something Greg had never been afraid of—especially if the rewards were great enough.

And he expected the rewards to be astounding. School was like a giant piggy bank, loaded with quarters. Greg was convinced that his new product would be like a hammer—the perfect hammer. He was going to crack the school wide open.

Chapter 4

UNITS

Standing in the cafeteria line, Greg opened his red plastic pencil case. He counted once, and then he counted again, just to be sure. Then he grinned. There were thirteen left.

Sweet! That means I sold seventeen units.

That's what Greg called the comic books he'd been selling—units. And selling seventeen units before lunch was a new sales record.

Greg's comic books weren't the kind for sale at stores. Regular comic books were sort of tall. Also a little floppy. Not Greg's.

Greg's comic books were about the size of a credit card, and they could stand up on one end all by themselves. They were only sixteen pages long, and he could fit about fifty of them into his pencil case. These comic books were short and sturdy. And that's why they were called Chunky Comics.

Greg loved that name. He had chosen it

himself. He got to pick the name because he was the author of all the Chunky Comics stories. He had drawn all the pictures too. And he was also the designer, the printer, and the binder. Plus he was the marketing manager, the advertising director, and the entire sales force. Chunky Comics was a one-kid operation, and that one kid was Greg Kenton.

Greg snapped the pencil case shut and grabbed a tray. He took a grilled cheese sandwich, a cup of carrot sticks, and then looked over the fruit cocktail bowls until he found one with three chunks of cherry. He got a chocolate milk from the cooler, and as he walked toward his seat, Greg did some mental math.

Monday, the first day Chunky Comics had gone on sale, he had sold twelve units; Tuesday, fifteen units; Wednesday, eighteen units; and today, Thursday, he had already sold seventeen units—before lunch. So that was . . . sixty-two units since Monday morning, and each little book sold for $.25. So the up-to-the-minute sales total for September 12 was . . . $15.50.

Greg knew why sales were increasing: word of mouth. Kids had been telling other kids about his comic book. The cover illustration was powerful, the inside pictures were strong, and the story was loaded with action. The title was *Creon: Return of the Hunter,* and it was volume 1, number 1, the very first of the Chunky Comics. So that made it a collector's item.

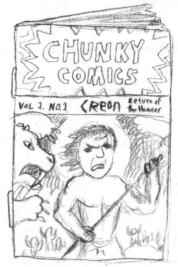

Greg sat down at his regular lunch table, next to Ted Kendall. Ted nodded and said, "Hi," but Greg didn't hear him. Greg picked up his sandwich and took a big bite. He chewed the warm bread and the soft cheese, but he didn't taste a thing. Greg was still thinking about sales.

Fifteen fifty in three and a half days—not so hot.

Greg had set a sales goal for the first week: twenty-five dollars—which meant that he had to sell one hundred units. It looked like he was going to fall short.

The idea of making and selling comic books had hit Greg like a 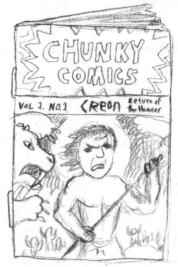 over the head from Superman himself. It made perfect sense.

Candy and gum were against school rules, and tiny toys were boring—and also against the rules. But how could he go wrong selling little books? School was all about books and reading. True, reading a comic book wasn't exactly the same as reading a regular book, but still, there was a rack of comics right in the kids section at the public library downtown, and some new graphic novels, too.

Comic books had been part of Greg's life forever, mostly because of his dad's collection. Batman, Superman, The Flash, Spider-Man, Marvel Classics, Uncle Scrooge, and all the Disney comics—his dad's collection filled three shelves in the family room—and it was worth over ten thousand dollars. Once Greg had shown he knew how to take care of the comic books, he had been allowed to read and look at them all he wanted. Greg had even bought a few collectible comics of his own, mostly newer ones that weren't very expensive.

It was his love of comic books that had first gotten Greg interested in drawing. Comics had led Greg to books like *How to Draw Comic-Book Villains*, *You Can Draw Superheroes*, *Make Your Own Comic-Book Art*, and *Draw the Monsters We Love to Hate*. Back in third grade Greg had used his own money to buy india ink, dip pens, brushes, and paper at the art supply store. And drawing new comic-book characters was one of his favorite things to do—when he wasn't earning money.

That whole summer before sixth grade Greg had worked toward the launch of Chunky Comics. From the start he had felt pretty sure he could come up with a story idea, and he knew he would be able to do the drawings.

But first he'd had to deal with a lot of *hows*: How does a whole comic book get put together? How big should each one be? How was he going to print them? How much would it cost him to make each one? And finally, how much money should he charge for his finished comic books—assuming he could actually make some?

But one by one, Greg had found the answers. An encyclopedia article about printing books had helped a lot. It showed how pages of a book start as one large sheet of paper that gets folded in half several times. Each time the sheet is folded, the number of pages is doubled. So Greg took a piece of regular letter-size paper, and folded it in half three times the way

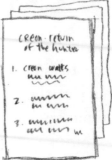

it showed in the encyclopedia. That one piece of paper turned into a chunky little sixteen-page book—Chunky Comics. It was so simple.

But not really. Greg figured out that making little comic books was a ten-step process:

1. Write a story that can be told on twelve to fourteen mini–comic book pages.

2. Sketch, draw, ink, and then letter all sixteen minipages—which include the front and back covers.

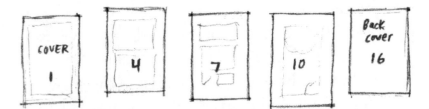

3. Paste eight of the minipage drawings into their correct positions on a piece of paper to make "master copy one"—a sheet that can be copied again and again.

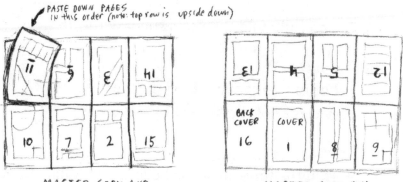

PASTE DOWN PAGES
IN this order (note: top row is upside down)

Master copy one grid (top row upside down): 11, 6, 3, 14; bottom row: 10, 7, 2, 15

MASTER COPY ONE

Master copy two grid (top row upside down): 13, 4, 5, 12; bottom row: BACK COVER 16, COVER 1, 8, 9

MASTER COPY TWO

4. Paste up the other eight minipages to make "master copy two."

5. Using a copier, print the images from "master copy one" onto one side of a "press sheet"—a piece of regular letter-size paper.

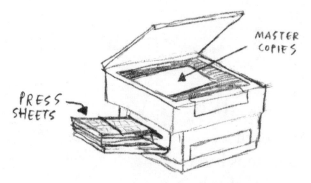

MASTER COPIES

PRESS SHEETS

6. Print "master copy two" onto the flip side of the press sheet—making eight page images on the front, and eight on the back.

7. Carefully fold the press sheet with the sixteen copied minipages on it.

8. Put in two staples along the crease at the very center of the little book—between pages 8 and 9.

9. Trim the three unstapled edges—and that makes one finished mini–comic book.

10. Repeat.

And each of the ten steps had to be done perfectly, or no one would ever want to spend money on his little comics.

After all the *hows* had been settled, then came the writing. But Greg hadn't written just one story. He had developed a master publishing plan. Volume 1 was going to be about Creon, an incredibly intelligent Stone Age hero who helped his tribe deal with ancient dangers, like prehistoric beasts and Cro-Magnon marauders. Greg figured there could be seven or eight issues about Creon.

Chunky Comics volume 2 would feature the future, where a superhero named Eeon tried to protect a small colony of humans living in a world of melting ice caps and mutant life-forms that were part human, part toxic sludge, and part recycled trucks and airplanes. Again, there would be seven or eight issues featuring Eeon.

Then Chunky Comics volume 3 would feature Leon, a fairly normal modern-age technodude who suddenly finds himself energized when his digital atomic watch overheats and burns its circuits into the nerves on his wrist. Leon learns that the watch can be set for the future or the past. The six or seven time-travel adventures of volume 3 would follow Leon to the past, where he would team up with Creon, and then to the future, where he would offer his services to the amazing Eeon. And eventually, all three characters would have some final episodes together: Creon, Leon, and Eeon—past, present, and future.

Once the master plan was set, writing the first Creon story, *Return of the Hunter,* had been pretty easy for Greg. But the drawing was more difficult than he'd thought it would be. It had taken a long time to get each small page looking just the way he wanted. It wasn't like doodling or sketching. These pictures had to be good—good enough to sell.

When both covers and the fourteen inside pages had been drawn and inked and pasted in place to make the two master copies, Greg tackled his first printing.

The copier he used was his dad's, and it was actually part of the printer that was hooked up to the computer in the family room. It was an ink-jet printer, plus a scanner, plus a copier—one of those "all-in-one" machines. It made copies in either black and white or color.

Greg had stuffed about forty ruined sheets of paper into the recycling bin before he had figured out how to get all sixteen page images copied correctly onto the front and back of one sheet of paper.

But finally, he had folded his first perfectly

printed sheet, stapled it twice, and trimmed the top, front, and bottom edges. And then, one hot night in the middle of July, Greg stood there in his family room and thumbed through the very first copy of the very first issue of the very first volume of Chunky Comics. It had been a proud moment.

Greg had done some record keeping along the way. He added up all the time, and learned some bad news: It had taken him more than sixty hours to make that very first comic book. But there was good news too, because it took him only two more hours to print, fold, staple, and trim the next one hundred copies of volume 1, number 1.

As he'd worked on his drawing skills over the summer, Greg had gotten better—and faster, too. Plus he'd had fun. He had dug out all his old drawing books, looking for shortcuts and new tips from the pros. Drawing was something he could do at night, so he still got to enjoy his days outdoors, and also do the regular summertime jobs that kept money coming in.

Drawing and inking the pictures for the next two comic books had only taken him about twenty hours—nine to eleven hours each. And by the time school began in September, Greg had the master copy pages for the next two Creon issues all put together and ready to print. Plus he had three hundred copies of *Return of the Hunter* printed, folded, stapled, trimmed, and ready to sell.

Making the comics had been fun, but Greg felt sure that selling them was going to be even better. If he kept the price at just a quarter per issue, the profits were still going to be fantastic. He had figured it all out. Ink for the copier was pretty expensive, but Greg had a kit for refilling the cartridges. All together, ink for one comic, plus one piece of paper, plus two staples cost him less than two cents. So, not counting his own time, selling one Chunky Comic book was like turning two pennies into a quarter. The money was going to come rolling in.

Digging around in the fruit cocktail on his lunch tray, Greg stabbed one of the cherry pieces with a fork. As he chewed the sweet fruit, Greg reviewed the sales figures again, and then shrugged. *Fifteen dollars and fifty cents—that's still not terrible. I mean, this is a brand-new business.*

All things considered, Greg decided that

Chunky Comics was off to a pretty good start. And before lunch was over, Greg had hired Ted to become the first sales agent for Chunky Comics, offering him a nickel for every two copies he sold. So Greg was still hoping to reach that goal of selling one hundred units the first week.

But business can be a lot like life—full of unexpected events. And thirty-three minutes later, standing in the hallway next to the music room, Greg and his new company got a shock.

There were two minutes left before sixth-grade chorus, and Greg was making the most of his time. He had just sold two copies of *Return of the Hunter* to Roy Jenkins when Ted came up and pressed something into his hand.

Greg glanced down and saw a minicomic. Then he noticed the expression on Ted's face. "What?" he asked. "Something wrong with this one?"

Ted nodded and said, "Take a look."

Greg turned the little book over. Ted was right. Something was *very* wrong with this one. Because what Greg held in his hand was not one of his Chunky Comics.

A tiny banner on the front cover announced that this was "An Eentsy Beentsy Book." The title was *The Lost Unicorn*, and the cutesy cover picture had been brightened up with colored pencil.

A deep scowl formed on Greg's face as he realized what he was holding. It was obvious: Some other kid was trying to cash in on *his* idea. And who was the person responsible for this . . . this sneak attack, this giant *rip-off*?

Greg didn't even have to look. He knew. Only one person would have dared to copy his idea like this. But Greg turned to the first page of the little book and looked anyway.

And there was the proof, in tiny, perfect cursive, just below the title: "Written and Illustrated by Maura Shaw."

Chapter 5

THE GIRL ACROSS THE STREET

Greg Kenton had always lived on Maple Avenue. As a very young boy, Greg had sometimes noticed the girl across the street who helped her dad rake leaves, and sometimes he had seen her riding a tricycle around and around on her driveway. She looked like she was about his age, but she didn't go to his nursery school or his Sunday school. So Greg didn't know who she was—and he didn't care.

Greg's world was small back then, and that little blond girl wasn't part of it. Greg noticed the girl the way he noticed the neighborhood dogs, or the colors of the flowers growing next to the front walk, or the blinking yellow light at the corner. Even when they both started kindergarten at the same school, Greg went in the morning, and the girl went afternoons. It was like they lived on different continents. The concrete ocean between them was only thirty-five feet wide, but young children never crossed it alone.

For his fifth birthday Greg got a Big Wheel, all blue and red and yellow with fat black tires. The hard plastic wheels made a huge rumbling sound, as loud as the trucks on Maple Avenue.

The first day he had it, Greg rode his Big Wheel for at least two hours. Over and over he rocketed down his driveway, yanked the handlebars to the right, and then roared along the sidewalk, his curly hair swept back from his high forehead. And when he noticed the girl across the street sitting on her front steps watching him, Greg poured on an extra burst of speed, and he smiled and waved as he went grinding by. The girl waved back, but she didn't smile.

Then late one afternoon about a week later, the little girl wasn't sitting on her steps when Greg went outside to ride. She was thundering around and around her driveway on a Big Wheel of her own—except hers was pink and green and white. And when Greg went speeding out of his driveway and zipped along the sidewalk, she did the same thing, a mirror image. And when Greg stopped at the corner of Tenth Street and headed back toward his driveway, so did the girl across the street. When he sped up, so did she. When he jammed his feet to the ground and slammed to a stop, she did too.

Greg was annoyed, but he pretended to ignore her. He turned and slowly pedaled up toward the corner at Tenth Street again. He didn't look, but he could tell by the sounds that the girl was doing the same thing over on her own sidewalk.

Greg turned his Big Wheel around and put his feet on the pedals. Then he looked across the street. The girl had turned her Big Wheel around too, and she looked back at him, smiling. And when Greg nodded, they both took off.

In seconds Greg was zooming along at top speed, legs pumping, hands tight around the plastic grips. The sidewalk sloped slightly downhill, and as he neared his house, Greg started to ease up. He had never gone down the block past his driveway before. But he glanced over and he could see that the girl wasn't slowing down. So Greg kept going, flying toward the corner where the tall blue mailbox stood. In the places where tree roots had lifted the sidewalk, Greg bounced up off his seat, barely able to keep control. At this speed, if he tried to turn the corner at Ninth Street, he'd flip over for sure. So at the last possible second, Greg dug his sneakers into the sidewalk and skidded to a full stop, his front wheel inches from the curb.

Looking quickly to the other side of Maple Avenue, Greg saw that the girl was stopped too, and also at the edge of the curb. And still smiling.

Greg shouted across the street, "It's a tie."

The girl shook her head and shouted back, "*Almost* a tie."

Greg frowned. "Want to race again?"

"Maybe tomorrow."

"Because you're scared, " Greg shouted.

The girl didn't answer him. She just kept smiling, turned her Big Wheel around, and started pedaling slowly up the street toward her driveway.

That was the first of many Big Wheel races, with each of them ending as a tie—or almost a tie.

And soon Greg had learned the name of the girl across the street: Maura Shaw.

Chapter 6

SOUR BUSINESS

Sometimes a disagreement between two kids stays that way—just between the kids themselves. But the clash between Greg and Maura had always been right out in the open, and it had deep historical roots. Their wrangling had been noticed by their parents, by their neighbors, by all their friends, and especially by every teacher who had ever had them in the same classroom.

"Greg and Maura squabble like cats and dogs all day long, always trying to outdo each other. My classroom's not big enough with those two around." That's how their first-grade teacher Mrs. Gibson had described the situation.

"Maura and Greg are both so headstrong. They have a definite personality conflict." That's what their fourth-grade teacher Mrs. Haversock had said about it.

"They're like positive and negative numbers, always trying to cancel each other out." That's how Mr. Zenotopoulous tried to explain it. Now that Greg and Maura were both in sixth grade, he was their math teacher.

And as Greg himself stood there outside the music room on Thursday afternoon, holding "An Eensty Beentsy Book," his long, thin face drawn into a fierce scowl, how did he describe his problem with Maura?

"I hate her *guts*!"

Strong words. It was an expression Greg had picked up from watching old gangster movies. And it was also a stupid expression. Because if Maura Shaw's guts had come walking down the hall, Greg wouldn't have recognized them. The truth is, all guts are pretty much alike.

But Greg was not thinking logically at that

moment. And saying that he hated Maura's guts did not feel like too strong a statement. If anything, it wasn't strong enough. Because as far as Greg was concerned, Maura was no better than a common thief. She had always been a copycat, which would have been bad enough. But Greg couldn't stand it when she tried to weasel in on his moneymaking ideas. Maura had been a bother for years. And now, *this*.

Greg stuffed Maura's book into his pocket just as the bell rang. He ducked into the music room and sat down. Mrs. Chalmers immediately began playing scales on the piano, and the class began singing warm-up exercises.

Greg had his mouth open, and his voice went "Oh-ee-oh-ee-oh-ee-oh-ee-ohhh" along with the others. But Greg's mind was elsewhere.

He had big plans for Chunky Comics—*huge* plans. And Maura was going to try to sell her stupid Eentsy Beentsy Books at school and try to steal his customers. Maura was going to eat into his profits, maybe even mess up everything. *Something* had to change—Maura, to be exact. And she had to change right away, like today.

But as Greg sifted through his past experiences with Maura, one particular incident jumped to mind, and it did not give him much reason to hope. . . .

Greg's first business outside his own home was a lemonade stand. He had sold his first cup of lemonade at the end of June during the summer after second grade, and he stuck with it every hot, sunny day all during July and August. The next summer he sold lemonade again, and his customers came back. The second summer he started using the honor system. People served themselves, and just dropped quarters through a slot in the lid of a glass jar. That left Greg free to make money doing something like mowing a lawn at the same time.

The first really hot day during the summer after fourth grade he set up shop once more. His new sign announced:

Less than an hour later the trouble began. Because there was Maura Shaw, right across the street, setting up her own lemonade stand under a bright beach umbrella with a big sign:

Maura's TASTY LEMONADE only 20¢

All afternoon Greg had watched helplessly. About half of *his* customers stopped and bought lemonade from Maura.

Two days later on a Saturday it got hot again, and by noon, there was Maura, sitting under her umbrella, selling bargain lemonade.

However, Greg had been thinking. He loaded an ice bucket and two jugs of lemonade onto a red wagon. Then he began pulling the wagon around the neighborhood, delivering cold cups of lemonade right into the sweaty hands of the people who were outside mowing and trimming and working in their gardens.

Direct delivery was a great idea, and some people bought two or three refills. Greg was making good money.

But twenty minutes later, there was Maura on the other side of the street pulling a wagon, selling her lemonade exactly the same way.

Greg had gotten furious. He looked both ways and then he'd marched across Maple Avenue and planted himself in front of Maura on the sidewalk.

She'd pushed a few strands of damp yellow hair up off her forehead. She looked Greg right in the eye and said, "You're in my way."

Greg shook his head. "No, you're in *my* way. *You're* the one who's stealing my customers—and my ideas."

Maura didn't blink. "I can sell lemonade if I want to. Anybody can. Like my mom. She sold lemonade when she was little. She told me so. And I can pull my wagon around anywhere I want to."

Then Maura had taken a step closer and put her freckled nose about three inches from Greg's, her eyes big and blue and absolutely fearless. "So get out of the way."

Maura probably outweighed him by fifteen

pounds back then, and Greg hadn't wanted to have a shoving match. So he'd moved off the sidewalk. But as her wagon went by, he had kicked the back wheel and said, "Why don't you try coming up with an idea of your own?"

Maura said, "Maybe I will," and she stuck out her tongue.

"Yeah," said Greg, "except you don't even have a brain."

"I do too."

"So prove it," said Greg.

"Maybe I will," Maura said again.

And Greg said, "I doubt it . . . brainless!"

For about a week after that, Maura didn't show up on the lemonade trail, and Greg had thought, *I guess I told* her! The weather stayed hot, and Greg had been making two, sometimes three or four dollars a day.

Then one afternoon he'd spotted Maura going from door to door around the neighborhood. She was wearing a yellow dress and white socks and little black shoes. And she was carrying something in a wooden picnic basket. Greg couldn't tell what Maura was selling, but he could see that money was changing hands. He had watched for about ten minutes, dying to know what she was up to. Finally he couldn't stand it.

Greg slipped out his side door, ran across the backyard, trotted down the alley, tiptoed between two houses, and hid in the bushes next to the Jansens' front porch. He'd had to wait almost ten minutes, crouched in the scratchy hemlock branches, swatting at mosquitoes. Then Maura had crossed the street and walked up the Jansens' front steps. Her feet on the wooden porch sounded like a bass drum. Greg heard the bell, then little footsteps came running, and someone bumped into the storm door.

Maura said, "Hi, Timmy. Is your mommy home?"

Timmy Jansen was about three. After a long pause he said, "She's *my* mommy."

Maura said, "Uh-huh . . . can you call your mommy for me?"

Another pause.

Timmy said, "She's *my* mommy."

Maura laughed and said, "I know, so just turn around and shout, 'Mommy—someone's at the door.' You can do that, right? So call her. . . . Go on, call her. Your mommy *is* at home, isn't she?"

Another long pause.

"She's *my* mommy."

Maura gave up, and she called through the screen, "Mrs. Jansen . . . Mrs. Jansen? It's me, Maura Shaw. Is anybody home?"

Greg had heard bigger footsteps, and then, "Oh, hello, Maura. Don't you look pretty today! It's not Girl Scout cookie time, is it?"

"No, I'm selling pot holders. I made them myself."

Over in the bushes, Greg had almost burst out laughing. *Pot holders? That is so dumb!*

Mrs. Jansen thought otherwise. "These are *beautiful*, Maura—so colorful. And you say you made them all by yourself?"

"Uh-huh."

"Well, I want these two for myself . . . and these blue-and-pink ones will go perfectly in my sister's kitchen. How much are you charging?"

"Two dollars each."

"Oooh—a bargain. I'm going to buy an *extra* pair for myself."

Greg heard Mrs. Jansen walk away, come back, and open the storm door. And

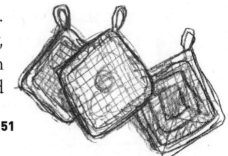

then Greg heard his favorite sound in all the world—the whisper of crisp bills as the money was counted out. Except the bills were being counted into Maura's open hand.

"Here's a five, and six, seven, eight, nine, ten, eleven . . . Would you mind taking four quarters?"

"Not at all."

Greg heard the coins, then Mrs. Jansen had said, "And that makes twelve dollars."

Maura said, "Thank you."

"And thank *you*, Maura. We'll think of you every time we use these pot holders in the kitchen, won't we, Timmy?"

And Timmy said, "She's *my* mommy."

Greg had heard enough. He slipped out of the bushes, scooted between the houses, and ran home.

It was hot, so he'd gone to the refrigerator and poured himself a glass of his leftover lemonade. It tasted sour.

Greg remembered grabbing a pencil and a memo pad so he could do some calculating. If Maura had gone all around the neighborhood, and if every mom who was home had bought a couple of pot holders, then . . . she might have

made as much as *fifty dollars*—in *one* afternoon! Fifty dollars was serious money.

Then the doorbell had rung, and his mom
had called from the basement, "Greg? Would
you see who's at the door?"

It was Maura.

She had smiled at Greg and said, "Hello,
little boy. Is your mommy at home?"

Greg glared at her. Then he'd grinned and
said, "She's *my* mommy."

Maura's blue eyes had gotten wide, and then
narrowed. She pointed an accusing finger and
said, "You were *spying* on me, over at the
Jansens'! Weren't you?"

Greg's grin got bigger, and again he'd said,
"She's *my* mommy."

Then—*whomp!*—he'd slammed the door in
Maura's face. It felt so good.

The bell rang again, and as he opened the
door for the second time, Greg called over his
shoulder, "Mom, there's . . . *something* at the
door. It's for you."

Greg's mom had bustled into the front
hallway. "Maura—I was hoping you'd be
coming. Mrs. Altman called and said you
were walking around selling the *prettiest* pot

holders. I hope you have some nice ones left for me."

Greg had gone up about four steps on the front-hall stairs and leaned against the banister so he could look over his mom's shoulder. There was a yellow cloth covering the bottom of the basket, and the pot holders were arranged so they looked like diamonds instead of squares.

"These are *lovely*, Maura. How much do they cost?"

Maura had hesitated half a second, and then she said, "Three dollars."

"*Three?*" Greg said. "I thought they were *two* dollars each."

But Maura had held her ground. "I've only got four left, and these are my best ones. These are three dollars each."

Greg had known exactly what Maura was doing. She was raising her prices, trying to discover the most a customer would actually pay. It was a smart thing to do—something Greg would have done himself.

And sure enough, his mom had said, "Only three dollars for a beautiful handmade pot holder? I'll take all four of them." And she'd gone to get her purse.

Maura had known she'd just won a battle. She'd looked up at Greg, given him a big smile, and said, "Still think I don't have a brain? I just made twelve dollars—*another* twelve dollars— right here at your house. Say . . . I'm thirsty." She'd pulled a quarter from the pocket of her dress and held it out to him. "Could you get me a cup of lemonade?"

Greg curled up his lip and said, "I wouldn't give you—" But just then his mom came back. He hadn't finished that sentence. He'd turned around, stomped up the stairs, then down the hall to his bedroom, and slammed the door.

Sitting there in the music room more than a year after the lemonade battles, Greg still remembered clearly what had happened next. He had walked over to his bedroom window and watched Maura walk across Maple Avenue to her front door, swinging her empty picnic basket as she pushed another twelve dollars into her dress pocket.

And he remembered thinking that making those pot holders and selling them to moms had been a smart idea. And getting dressed up, and putting that nice cloth in the bottom of the basket? Also smart.

And Greg remembered that he'd had to admit that the girl he had called "brainless" was actually a good thinker. Maura *did* have a brain. And not backing down when he had caught her charging three dollars per pot holder instead of two? That had taken some guts.

And remembering that Maura had guts reminded Greg how much he hated them.

Maura was a tough competitor. And in another thirty-five minutes, he'd see her, because they were both in level-four math.

It was time for a showdown.

Chapter 7

ORDER AND CHAOS

Ashworth Intermediate School was a big outfit, and when you put four hundred and fifty kids, mostly between the ages of nine and twelve, under one roof, a certain amount of hubbub and clutter is normal. And therefore, room 27 was not normal.

Room 27 at Ashworth School was never messy, never loud. Room 27 was always like a peaceful island, an oasis of order and calm. That's because the small kingdom known as room 27 was controlled by Mr. Anthony Zenotopoulous, who, for obvious reasons, was known simply as Mr. Z.

Mr. Z was a man of average size, except perhaps for his head, which seemed a bit too large for his body. But that might have been an optical illusion caused by the burst of black and gray hair spiraling out one or two inches in all directions. Apart from his unruly

hair, Mr. Z dressed neatly, but not formally. He wore a coat and tie only for the end-of-year assembly. The rest of the time he wore khakis or corduroys and loose-fitting collared shirts, carefully ironed. He had piercing dark eyes and a bright smile, which made it harder to notice the large nose that lived between them.

Mr. Z taught sixth graders, and in his kingdom, mathematics ruled. Everything about his room—including its legendary calmness—was a function of math. Mr. Z did not just *teach* sixth-grade math. He lived math. He breathed and ate and slept and dreamed math. His wife taught geometry at the high school, so you could even say that he had married math—

plus their only son was an engineering major at the state university.

For Mr. Z math was the source of all that was beautiful, good, and true. Math controlled the orbits of the planets, always in perfect, stressless balance. Math was frictionless. Math supplied the principles that sent rockets past the moon and helped Beethoven create his symphonies. Mr. Z believed that even the smile of the Mona Lisa, like the spiral of the chambered nautilus, could be expressed as a ratio, a set of elegant numbers.

The alarm clock, the thermometer, the calendar, the digital watch on his wrist, the odometer in his car, the test and quiz scores of his students, the percentage points of his grading scale—these gave him the numbers he lived by. He awoke each day at 6:15, school or no school. Channel 7's weather forecasts were the most accurate—he'd done a three-year study himself—so a predicted high temperature of seventy degrees or warmer = khaki pants + a short-sleeved shirt; sixty-nine degrees or below = corduroys + long sleeves; and for a high temperature of forty degrees or lower, + one sweater.

Mr. Z put his heavy down coat into storage on March 1, and got it out again on October 1. He had an appointment at the barber shop every third Thursday at 4:15 p.m. He changed the oil in his white Toyota Camry every 5,500 miles, and when the odometer reached 110,000 miles—the twentieth oil change—he and his wife began shopping for a new white Camry. Why a Camry? Math: The Camry was the car that cost the *least* amount of dollars, had the *most* features he could afford, and had the *fewest* service problems. Why white? Again, math: White was the color that kept the inside temperature of a car *lowest* in the summer—when running the air conditioner meant buying *more* gas and getting *fewer* miles per gallon.

There were 185 school days per year, and 55 minutes in each class period. Mr. Z wrote the number of remaining minutes of math class on the board at the start of each school day—beginning at 10,175. Quiz scores counted once, and test scores counted twice. Grade percentages were calculated out to three decimal places, then rounded up. And arguing about grades was pointless: Numbers never lied.

Mr. Z had a sense of humor, but it was a

mathematical sense of humor. He wasn't witty or clever, but he had an almost endless supply of math puns. What did the triangle say to the circle? Your life seems so pointless. What did the ninety-degree angle say to the ninety-one-degree angle? Don't be obtuse. What did the plus sign say to the minus sign? You're always so negative. Why didn't the rectilinear equilateral like jazz? He was a square. And so was Mr. Z.

If Mr. Z seemed stiff, or set in his ways, or rigid in his views, that was a function of math as well. In math there were fixed rules. Math involved pure operations that required no bending, no guesswork, no emotional adjustments— only the glide and flow of intelligence. There were always answers, *right* answers, and it was possible to understand exactly what was right about them.

And that's why Mr. Z loved math—*loved*, not liked, not enjoyed, not appreciated. Loved. He loved thinking about math, he loved using it, and most of all, he loved teaching it. Math was perfect. Math clarified the jumbled minds and disciplined the untidy lives of his students. So many things changed constantly—politics, weather, the price of energy, the cover of *Time* magazine. Not math. As he told his students, "Now and forever, two plus two will *always* equal four—every single day."

But on this particular day, with 9,790 minutes of math class remaining in his sixth-grade year, Greg Kenton came stomping into the orderly world of room 27 with a head full of chaos. He walked straight over to Maura Shaw. He slapped the Eentsy Beensty Book down onto her desk, and through clenched teeth he said, "Nice! Nice rip-off! You are *such* a *thief*. You *stole* my idea, and you know it. So stop it. Stop it *now!*"

Maura jumped up, nose to nose with Greg. "Oh, sure, like you invented paper and drawings—and words, too, right? Just so you know, anybody can make anything they want to. And they can sell stuff too. It's a free country—like, for over two hundred years—or hadn't you heard?"

Mr. Z looked up from his grade book, saw the disturbance in aisle four, and got to his feet. Speaking as he moved, he was at the scene in three seconds.

"All right, all right there . . . easy does it.

Greg, lower your voice. Maura, you too. And sit down. Now what's this about?"

"Simple." Greg opened his pencil case and said, "I started making these great little comic books, and now she's ripping me off with her stupid imitation. She's using *my* idea, and it's like she's stealing money right out of my pocket." He pointed at the unicorn book on her desk. "*That's* what this is about."

Maura shook her head. "What it's about is that you're a greedy little money-grubber, just like always—'Mine, all mine.' That's all you ever care about!"

"That's a lie!"

"All right," said Mr. Z, "calm down."

But Maura was on her feet again. "It's true! And poor wittle Gweg can't stand it when somebody else has a good idea."

Greg snorted, and grabbed the Eentsy Beentsy Book. "Yeah, right! Like *this* is a good idea. You know what this is? Garbage! Cheap, stupid garbage—just like you!" And Greg ripped the front cover off *The Lost Unicorn* and threw it at Maura's face.

"*Both* of you—*stop* this! Just *stop* it!"

It was like Mr. Z had disappeared. All Maura could see was her little book as Greg began to tear off another page.

"Give me that!" She swung her right arm to grab for it, and Greg yanked the book up above his head. And as Maura's hand followed the moving book, the bottom three knuckles of her right hand connected with a sharp *crack* against the left side of Greg's nose.

Greg's mouth dropped open. So did Mr. Z's—and Maura's.

There was a half-second of stunned silence, and then, "OWWW!" Greg clutched his nose, which began to bleed, dripping onto Maura's desk.

Room 27, usually quieter than the library, flashed to life.

"Did you see that?!"

"What? Where?"

"Maura . . . she *pounded* him!"

"No way!"

"I saw it—look at his nose."

"Ooh, *blood*!"

And amid all the other noise, Maura squeaked out, "Oh . . . oh . . . I'm really sorry . . . I didn't mean . . .

I didn't mean to . . . really, I didn't . . ."

Mr. Z wanted to take charge. He wanted to quiet the room, calm Maura, and get Greg to the nurse. But there was blood.

Numbers never bleed, which Mr. Z believed was one of their best qualities. Because just the word *blood* was enough to make him start looking for a chair so he could sit and put his head between his knees.

Mr. Z turned away from Greg. Already woozy, his face was going gray, but as he slumped into the nearest empty desk, swallowing hard, he managed to say, "Maura . . . please help . . . Greg . . . to the nurse. I'll . . . I'll be . . . here."

Maura rushed to the front of the room, yanked five or six tissues from the box on Mr. Z's desk, and hurried back to Greg. "Here."

Greg accepted the tissues, but when Maura took his elbow and began steering him toward the hallway, he jerked his arm free and made his own way out the door. It was bad enough he'd just gotten a bloody nose from a girl. No way was he going let that same girl turn around and help him.

Maura stopped at the doorway of the nurse's

office, and Mrs. Emmet took charge. Sitting Greg on the black vinyl cot, she grabbed a plastic cold pack from a cabinet and smacked it on her desk three or four times to activate the crystals. She pulled on a pair of pale green gloves, took a paper towel, got it wet at the sink, and began to clean up Greg's face.

"Lean forward." The nurse took the cold pack and wrapped it in a damp washcloth. Leaning over, she looked at the marks on Greg's skin, and then pressed the cold pack gently against his face.

Mrs. Emmet said, "How'd this happen?"

It would have been so easy for Greg to lift his bloody hand, point a crimson finger, and shout, "Maura did it! She slugged me right in the nose—hard!" He could have yelled so loud that the principal across the hall would have heard him.

But he didn't. He mumbled, "It was an accident. Somebody grabbed for something . . . and I got in the way."

The nurse lifted the cold pack and touched Greg's nose carefully with her gloved fingers. He flinched. Mrs. Emmet said, "Hmm . . . It's not broken, but you're going to have a black eye—a real prizewinner. You need to stay here till I'm sure the bleeding has stopped." She pressed the cold pack back in place and said, "Put your left hand here, and press . . . not too hard."

Greg did as he was told.

Turning to the doorway, Mrs. Emmet said, "Maura, did any blood get on you?"

Maura looked at her hands and down her front. She shook her head.

"Anywhere else?" asked the nurse. "Where did this happen?"

"In Mr. Z's room. Some drops got on a desk, and maybe on the floor."

Mrs. Emmet nodded. "I'll send the custodian with disinfectant. You should get back to class now."

Maura hesitated. It was nice Greg hadn't blamed her, and she wanted him to turn and look at her. She wanted at least to nod a "thanks" at him. But Greg kept his eyes shut. So Maura turned and left.

Mrs. Emmet said, "Greg, I have to go find the custodian. You can lean back on those pillows now, but stay still, all right?" And she was gone.

The whole side of Greg's face throbbed as

he eased himself back. *Great—a black eye. From a girl. Just what I always wanted.*

What Maura had said in Mr. Z's room came back to him: ". . . you're a greedy little money-grubber, just like always!" Those words hurt— worse than his nose. His big brothers had been calling him stingy and greedy for years. *Is that what they all think, that I'm a money-grubber? Everybody wants a lot of money, right? What's wrong with that? Can I help it if I have good ideas? And that I'm willing to work? There's nothing wrong with that.*

Greg became aware that he had something clutched in his right hand. He brought it up where he could see it. It was the wad of bloody tissues. And something else—Maura's mini-book, *The Lost Unicorn.*

The front cover was half gone, and some of the wrinkled pages were streaked with blood.

 *Illustrated in living color,* Greg thought, and that made him smile, which forced a sharp pain up through his nose and left eye.

He got the book in focus, and using only his right hand, he began to turn the pages.

Greg could tell right away that it wasn't his

kind of story, which did not come as a surprise. It was about a young unicorn who'd gotten lost, also not a surprise. At first the unicorn was terrified, but then she remembered what her mother and father had told her: "If you ever have a problem, find someone with a bigger problem, and offer to help. Do this, and your own worries will disappear." So the unicorn went looking for someone to help, and found a princess who had been kidnapped, locked in a tower by a wicked ogre. The unicorn used her horn to chop down a tree, which leaned against the tower and gave the princess a way to escape. Then the unicorn gave the princess a ride back to her mother's castle. The queen was so happy to have her daughter back that she asked ten of her best knights to help the unicorn find her way home. And they all lived happily ever after.

Even though it seemed like a lame story to him, Greg had to admit that the writing was good. And the artwork wasn't bad either. It was actually a tiny picture book, not at all like a comic book. Each of Maura's pictures took up a whole page. There were no sequenced panels, no page grids, and no speech balloons like comics have. Still, the drawings were good. And Maura had drawn vines and flowers around the borders of each page.

Bringing the little book closer to his good eye, Greg blinked. Then he rubbed his finger on the page. The dark gray lines smudged and smeared. He could not believe what he was seeing. *It is—this is original artwork! Maura is drawing every book by hand and putting them together one at a time! No wonder she went nuts when I started ripping this one up!*

Leaning his head back and closing both eyes, Greg smiled. He'd just made an important dis-covery. This meant that Maura did not know how to mass-produce her books. It meant that she had probably made only four or five of them, tops. And it meant that at her current skill level as a minibook producer, she was just messing around—hardly a serious competitor. Maura wasn't even in the minor leagues.

And as his business mind clicked away, Greg saw the future grow bright again, with kids buying so many of his Chunky Comics that he would make tons of money. He would have to start getting his comics printed professionally. He'd have to hire a staff of artists to keep up with the increasing demand, maybe rent a building—or buy one. He'd start a Web site, and start selling to the major comics distributors, too. Eventually he'd have to open branch offices in New York, Chicago, Los Angeles—Hong Kong and London, too: Chunky Comics International. He'd get so rich that he could have a different limo for every day of the week, each with a comic-book hero painted on the hood.

Bbrrrrnnnnnng! Greg sat straight up, completely fuddled. He blinked. A cold pack lay on his arm, his head hurt, and he was on the cot in the nurse's office. Then the events of the day tumbled back into his memory. He'd been sound asleep.

Mrs. Emmet smiled at him from her desk. "Feeling better?"

"Yeah, a little." Greg leaned back again, reaching for the cold pack.

But then he made himself sit up. "Actually, I feel a lot better. So I guess I should get to my next class."

Greg had work to do. One more class period and Thursday would be history. He had comics to sell.

Maura came to the doorway. "Hi. I brought your backpack. And your pencil case. Your face looks better."

Greg didn't know what to say, so he just nodded.

Maura said, "You going to class?"

Greg looked at Mrs. Emmet. "Can I?"

She nodded. "You should be fine. But if you feel uncomfortable, come back, all right?"

"Okay." Greg stood up and walked to the door. "Thanks."

"You're welcome."

Maura gave Greg his things. He swung his backpack onto one shoulder, tucked the pencil case under his other arm, and headed down the long hallway toward the gym.

Maura turned and walked beside him. "So," she said, "you've got gym now?"

"Nope." Greg picked up his pace.

Maura matched him, step for step. "Language arts?"

"No . . . art."

Greg walked so fast that Maura almost had to trot to keep up. "Hey," she said, "before I forget—you have to go to Mr. Z's room after school."

Still walking, Greg glanced at her. "How come?"

"He wants to talk to you. And me, too. About what happened."

"Great," said Greg. "I'll be late for soccer."

Maura said, "Should you run around today? I mean, with your eye and everything?"

Greg stopped short and swung to face her. "Look. It's none of your business. It was just a little poke in the nose, all right? I'm okay, and I don't need you to tell me what to do."

"Fine," said Maura. "Do whatever you want. I don't care."

"Good, 'cause I don't care if you don't care. So go away."

"Don't worry, I'm going. Here," and Maura pushed a quarter into his hand. "This is yours."

"What's this for?" he asked.

"One of your comics—they're a quarter, right?"

"What . . . you sold one?"

"No," said Maura, "I bought one."

"*You?*"

"That's right." Maura stuck her chin out. "Any law against that?"

"No," said Greg. "But . . . why?"

73

"That's a stupid question. I read it. In math class. It's good."

Creative pride won a small victory over ill temper. Greg smiled. "You liked it? Really?"

Maura nodded. "Yeah, it was okay. But—" The bell rang. "Oops—I *can't* be late." Maura turned and dashed for class.

"'But' what?" Greg called after her.

"Later," she called back.

And Greg thought, *Later? Oh yeah. 'Cause we have to go see Mr. Z.*

The art room was close, and Greg quickly forgot Maura's comments about his comic book. He had to finish a wire sculpture. The thing was due Monday, and it was going to take a small miracle to get it done on time.

Still, that didn't keep Greg from selling three more copies of *Return of the Hunter* before the end of art class.

Chapter 8

TWO DOWN

When Greg got to Mr. Z's room after school on Thursday, no one else was there. He sat at a desk in the front row and looked over at the clock. It was already 3:05. Greg thought, *Six minutes. If he's not here in six minutes, I'm going to soccer.*

A minute later Maura burst into the room. "Sorry, I know I'm late, but I—" Then she saw only Greg was there. She stopped and then walked to the front of the room. "I thought I was late."

"You *are* late," said Greg. He jerked a thumb toward Mr. Z's desk. "Just not as late as *he* is."

Maura sat down a few seats away and turned to look out the windows.

A minute went by. The empty school felt too quiet to Greg. He said, "Um . . . so what's he want to say to us anyway?"

Without turning her head, Maura said, "Three guesses."

"Right," said Greg.

Then he remembered what Maura had said about his comic book: . . . *it was okay, but—*

Greg wanted Maura to finish that sentence. Then he thought, *What do I care what she thinks?*

But after another minute of silence, his curiosity won out. Still, he didn't want Maura to think he actually *cared* what she thought.

Then he hit on a way to bring up the subject. Greg said, "I read your unicorn book. It was good . . . for what it is."

Maura turned to face him, arching one of her pale eyebrows. "What's that supposed to mean?"

"Nothing," said Greg. "It's not really my kind of story, that's all—you know, princesses and unicorns. I like comic books. And your book isn't a comic."

"So why did you read it?"

Greg shrugged. "It was the only reading material I had in the nurse's office. I was bored. How come you read *my* story?"

Maura tossed her head. "Same reason.

There wasn't anything better to do in math."

"But you *bought* a copy of mine—*and* you said it was good, right?"

"Yeah," Maura admitted, "but . . ."

That's what Greg had been waiting for. "'But' what? What didn't you like about it?"

Maura was quiet a moment, and when she spoke, Greg saw she was choosing her words carefully. "Well, it's sort of like what you said about my book, about it not being your kind of story? See, I know you want to try to sell a lot of copies—"

Greg interrupted, "Because you think I'm a greedy little money-grubber, right?"

Maura's eyes flashed. "Can you just listen?"

Greg nodded, and Maura continued. "*I* liked the story, and I liked the artwork, too. But I don't think many other girls would. And since half the kids at school are girls, if you write boy stories, you're only going to sell half as many books as you could."

Greg pretended to look shocked, and then shook a finger at Maura. "'Boy stories'? I'm going to tell Mrs. Sanborn what you said." Mrs. Sanborn was their social studies teacher, and she talked a lot about equal rights for women—and girls. She got furious whenever someone suggested that men and women or boys and girls should be treated differently.

Maura said, "Don't be dumb. I'm not talking about equal rights. I'm talking about what girls like. And boys. And no matter what Mrs. Sanborn says, most boys don't pick stories about princesses, and most girls don't pick stories about cavemen with spears."

As Maura finished that sentence, Mr. Z walked in. "Cavemen with spears? Are you two calling each other names again?"

Maura and Greg shook their heads, and Mr. Z said, "Good. I was delayed in the office. I was afraid I'd get here and find you two wrestling on the floor or throwing chairs at each other. But you're not name-calling and not fighting. Looks like progress." He pulled a front-row desk forward a few feet, turned it around, and sat down midway between them.

Mr. Z had been planning what he would say to Greg and Maura all afternoon. He already knew exactly where he wanted this meeting to end up, but he was prepared to take his time getting there. In his mind it was like a math problem: He would add right ideas, subtract wrong ones, divide fuzzy thinking by pure logic, and then he and the chil-  dren would nod and smile at one another as peace and understanding multiplied itself.

Looking first into Maura's face and then into Greg's, Mr. Z said, "Now, tell me precisely what started that mess during sixth period. Greg, you first."

Greg took a deep breath and then let it out slowly. "Well, it really started at the end of lunch period. That's when I found out Maura was selling little books like mine, ripping me off."

"I did *not* rip you off!"

"Maura—" Mr. Z raised a warning finger. "Quiet. Your turn's coming."

Maura nodded, but kept on talking. "He just said a minute ago that my story is *nothing* like his!"

"Yeah," said Greg, his voice rising, "but it's still a minibook, right? Admit it—you ripped me off!"

"QUIET! Both of you!" Mr. Z was not used to raising his voice. "I am *not* going to put up with this. If you two can't talk this out with me, then I'll turn the whole matter over to Mrs. Davenport. And your parents." He looked from Maura to Greg and then back again. "Is that clear? Now I asked Greg to speak first. Maura, not another word."

Turning to Greg, he said, "So you found out Maura had these booklets for sale, and you got mad. Anything else?"

"Well," said Greg, "just that it didn't seem fair. It was *my* idea. So, yeah, I got mad. And I came to class that way, and . . . you saw the rest. And that's all."

Mr. Z nodded and said to Greg, "Okay. Now it's your turn to listen—not one word." Turning to Maura, he said, "Let's hear your side."

Maura shrugged. "There's not much to tell. I mean, what did *I* do? I was sitting here in class, and he comes blasting in and starts shouting and throwing stuff in my face. And me hitting him? That was an accident—he said so himself, to the nurse. So *I* didn't do anything."

"Pfffhh!" Greg pushed a puff of air between his lips—not a word, but close enough to draw a glare from the math teacher.

Mr. Z turned back to Maura. "Show me your little book. Do you have one?"

Maura zipped open a pocket on the front of her backpack, pulled out a copy of *The Lost Unicorn,* and handed it to Mr. Z. He quickly turned the pages, scanning the text and looking at the pictures.

Then turning to Greg, he asked, "And how about yours?" Greg took a copy from his pencil case and handed it over. Again Mr. Z did a skim.

Looking up from Creon's face to Greg's, he said, "So even though these are clearly very different items, you're still mad that Maura did something similar, right? Used the same idea?"

Greg nodded. "Right. My idea."

Looking Greg in the eye, Mr. Z said, "So you agree with me that a little book with pictures is an idea?"

"Yeah," said Greg, "of course. Like I said. It was my idea."

Mr. Z shook his head. "That's not what I said. I said, a little book with pictures is *an* idea—not that it is *your* idea." Then, holding up both minibooks between his thumb and index finger, he said, "These two different things are still just *one* idea. Right?"

Greg nodded. "Right, and the idea was mine. First."

Mr. Z leaned forward. "But the thing about a true idea is that no one can really own it— even the person who uses it first. In mathematics the Sumerians were the first to use the idea of place value—over five thousand years ago. But they do not *own* that idea. And when you sit here in my room adding large numbers, and you carry tens or hundreds over into the next place column, does a Sumerian come running into the room and say, 'Hey—quit it! That's *my* idea!'"

Greg didn't answer. He lowered his eyes and stared at a smear of green gum on the floor.

Mr. Z went on. "Now, if Maura had used your character, this Creon guy, or if she had made her drawings look just like yours, then I think you'd have more reason to be upset. But she didn't do that. She used an old idea—a small book—in her own way. And yes, she might have seen you do it first. But that's the way ideas work. They spread. So I don't think you should be mad at Maura. If anything, you should feel flattered. Someone thought the way you used an old idea was so new and interesting, that she wanted to try it out for herself."

Mr. Z paused.

Greg was looking down at his feet, studying his sneakers. He'd decided to just let Mr. Frizzyhead talk himself out. Why argue? The sooner this guy finished yakking, the sooner he could leave for soccer practice.

"Look at me, Greg."

Greg tipped his head back. He flicked his eyes to the teacher's face and then back to the floor. The math teacher said, "Is any of this making sense to you?"

Greg shrugged. "Sure. I guess so."

"Then I think all this adds up to one thing." Mr. Z paused, waiting for Greg to look him in the face. It didn't happen, so he said. "Greg, you need to apologize to Maura."

Greg's head jerked up. "Apologize? *Me?* No. No way."

Maura knew how stubborn Greg was, and she'd liked the talk they'd been having before the teacher had arrived. She quickly said, "It's okay, Mr. Z. He doesn't have to apologize."

Mr. Z said, "Yes, he *does*. First he has to apologize to you, and then he has to apologize to me for making a huge disturbance in my room and wasting precious class time. And all because of a comic book."

Greg felt the fury rising in his chest. He wanted to tip his head back and howl like Creon. He wanted to get up close to this man's huge nose and shout, "*I'm* the guy with the black eye here. *I'm* the one who's had his idea ripped off. Apologize? That is so *stupid*—no, actually, *you're* stupid!" Greg felt his face getting red, felt his heart pounding.

And then, for the second time in one day, Greg felt his nose begin to bleed. Only this time it was a real gusher. Blood streamed out his left nostril, over his lips, and dripped off his chin, spattering his shirt and the desk.

Mr. Z put one hand over his mouth and with the other, he pointed a shaky finger, his eyes wide. "Oh . . . oh. Your nose. It's . . . it's . . ." But he couldn't say the *b* word.

Mr. Z's face went pale as paper. Sweat stood out on his forehead, and behind the hand still covering his mouth, his breath came in gasps.

Earlier, Greg hadn't noticed Mr. Z's reaction to blood. This time he couldn't miss it. And he decided to enjoy it.

Greg leaned forward and nodded at Mr. Z,

making no effort to stop the flow. "Yes, my nose is bloody, very bloody. It's bleeding, and blood is getting all over the place—bloody, bloody, blood."

Mr. Z turned away, almost throwing up.

"Greg!" Maura snapped. "*Stop* it! That's *mean*." She'd already grabbed the tissues from the teacher's desk. "Here." And she pushed the box into Greg's hands.

Turning to Mr. Z, she said, "Can I get you something . . . some water?"

Mr. Z shook his head. "I . . . just need to . . . lie down." And with Maura to steady him, he eased out of the desk and onto the floor, flat on his back, eyes closed.

"Now you," Maura said to Greg. "Sit on the floor and lean forward. And squeeze your nose. Hard." Greg followed orders, but then decided he'd be more comfortable lying down.

Maura said, "I'll get the nurse. And a cold pack—two cold packs."

And she left Greg and Mr. Z littering the floor of room 27.

Chapter 9

APOLOGIES

Greg lay on his back, completely still. Even with one nostril plugged, he picked up the oily scent left over from last night's dust mopping. He watched the second hand on the big wall clock and listened to Mr. Z's deep breaths. His math teacher was also stretched out on the floor, about ten feet away.

And Greg thought, *Now I'm completely sunk. This guy is gonna ruin me.* And then another, deeper voice said, *Yeah, and I deserve it.* And Greg knew that second voice was telling the truth.

He said, "Mr. Z?"

In a voice so weak it was hard to hear, Mr. Z said, "Yes?"

"I'm sorry, about the blood stuff—after I saw it made you sick. Maura's right . . . it was mean. So I'm sorry."

Mr. Z was quiet, and then he said, "I know

it's irrational, my reaction to . . . that. It's only a liquid . . . and only a word. But seeing it, and hearing that word, and thinking about it—it gets me, every time."

Greg thought a moment. He said, "With me, it's snakes." And lying there on the floor, Greg shivered. "I don't even like pictures of them."

Mr. Z said, "Ah, yes—pictures. When I was in junior high, I thought I wanted to be a doctor. I went to the public library and found a medical textbook. It had pictures. That was the end of my medical career." He took a deep breath and let it out slowly. "Irrational. Anyway, apology accepted."

After a moment Mr. Z said, "What about the other matter, losing your temper over the little books? Any apologies for that?"

Greg didn't say anything.

Mr. Z said, "Earlier, when I told you I was delayed in the office? I was looking through your student file. And Maura's. You two have quite a history of conflict. And I thought I was going to be the big problem solver. I thought getting you to apologize would be a help. For both of you."

Greg turned his head to look at Mr. Z,

moving a little so the legs of the desks didn't block his view. The teacher had his eyes shut, and his face still looked pale. "But you don't understand," Greg said. "About my comic books, I mean. I worked all summer. It's like this whole business I'm trying to start, and it'll make *tons* of money. And at the start of math class I was thinking Maura would mess it all up."

"What—you don't think that anymore?" asked Mr. Z.

"Not really," said Greg. "I got a better look at her minibook. She's drawing all her pictures by hand, making her books one at a time."

"And you're not."

"No," said Greg. "I make one original, and then print the rest using a copier."

"Ah—," said Mr. Z. "Mass production, economies of scale, increased profits, and market dominance, right?"

Greg only understood about half of that, but he said, "Right. I can make forty or fifty copies in an hour, and the materials cost around two cents per copy. Then I sell each one for a quarter. And I've got about twenty more comics all planned out."

Mr. Z opened his eyes and turned his head

to look at Greg. "You see that? Talking was good. Helped me understand. So why didn't you just talk to Maura?"

Greg shrugged. "Because she's so . . . annoying."

Mr. Z's eyes drifted to the blood on Greg's shirt, and he quickly turned his eyes to the ceiling. He said, "I've got a theory about why you two keep fighting. You're both very much alike. And you're each too stubborn to take a step toward being friends."

Greg wasn't sure what to say to that, and while he was thinking, Maura came back into the room with the principal right behind her.

Mrs. Davenport said, "My goodness! Looks like an emergency room in here! A bleeder and a fainter come face-to-face—what are the odds of that? If we can patch up the math teacher, he can run the numbers and figure that out." She chuckled. "Mrs. Emmet's gone, so I'm your nurse, like it or not."

She went to Greg first and handed him a cold pack. "Maura tells me you already know what to do with this."

Greg nodded and pressed the blue plastic bag against his nose.

The principal gave a towel and a cold pack to Mr. Z, then she pulled a desk closer and lifted his feet onto the seat. "Get the feet above the head—that's first aid for big, strong swooning victims." Mrs. Davenport chuckled again. Mr. Z did not.

The principal said, "Greg, I've already called your mother, and she'll meet you at home. Maura's mother is coming in about five minutes, and she's driving you both."

Then she turned to Maura and said, "Would you go to the girls' room across the hall for me? Wet paper towels. We've got to get Greg cleaned up so that Mr. Zenotopoulous can get up off the floor. Or . . . we could just wait until it gets dark and all the *b-l-o-o-d* becomes invisible." She chuckled, and then said, "Sorry about the jokes. I'm just relieved this isn't more serious." Then turning back to Mr. Z, she said, "And I know all the other teachers will also be relieved when I tell them all about it tomorrow." More chuckles.

Greg had never heard Mrs. Davenport make a joke before, had not known such a thing was possible. And lying there on the floor, Greg thought, *Mr. Z's gonna get teased by the teachers tomorrow because blood makes him faint. And I'm gonna get teased by the kids because I got a black eye from a girl.*

Mrs. Davenport used the wet paper towels to clean up Greg's face, and then the desk and floor. It was a big mess, and before she was done, Maura had to go back for more supplies.

"All right, Greg, up you get . . . slowly . . . and keep your head steady." Mrs. Davenport helped Greg to his feet and then into a desk. "Stay put while Maura waits for her mother out front. I've got to get back to the office. Mr. Zenotopoulous, will you be all right for another few minutes—or shall I call for an ambulance?"

Greg could hear her chuckling as she walked away. He looked down at Mr. Z and said, "Does she always joke around like that with teachers? 'Cause she's not like that with kids."

Mr. Z smiled weakly. It didn't seem proper to talk about Mrs. Davenport with a student, so he said, "Most teachers have a sense of humor—and that includes principals."

Greg stared down at his blue-and-white soccer shirt, now streaked with blood. Greg thought, *Red, white, and blue—very patriotic.* He moved the desk so Mr. Z wouldn't be able to see his front. And then he thought of a question.

"So, Mr. Z, do you wish sometimes that you could have been a doctor? Like you said? Or maybe some other job like that? I mean instead of just being a teacher. Because if you'd been a doctor, you'd probably be really rich by now. Doctors make *so* much money. You know Ed McNamara? His dad's a doctor, and they're *super*rich."

Mr. Z did not want to discuss his personal life. He just laughed a little and said, "My older brother's a doctor, and he's not rich."

"Really?" Greg was surprised. "How come? "

"Because he lives in a part of Idaho where

they needed a good doctor but there wasn't a lot of money to pay for one."

Greg said, "So how come your brother doesn't move to Chicago, or Florida, or someplace like that?"

Mr. Z shrugged. "We haven't talked about it much, but I know he likes where he lives, and he likes his work there. He's not rich, but he certainly has enough. And for him, enough is enough."

Greg said, "Well, I guess that's okay for some people, but *I* want to be really, really rich. I'm going to make millions and millions."

"Hmm," said Mr. Z. "And what's all this money going to be used for?" he asked.

"Money?" Greg looked at Mr. Z as if he was an alien. "What's all the *money* for? To buy stuff. To go places and get whatever I want. And to do anything I want to. That's what the money's for."

Mr. Z said, "So if you had all the money you wanted, what would you do?"

Greg shrugged. "Anything I wanted to. I could do . . . anything."

Mr Z nodded. "Right, but give me an example."

"Okay," said Greg. "Like the house we live in now, my parents' house? It's not very big. Four bedrooms, two bathrooms, a basement playroom, a family room—just a regular house. So if I had enough money, I'd buy a house with something like ten bedrooms. And fifteen bathrooms. And two swimming pools, and this huge entertainment center with a home theater and surround sound and bass boosters. And a pool table. And air hockey too. Stuff like that."

Mr. Z raised his eyebrows. "Hmm. Interesting."

It was the way Mr. Z said *Interesting*, something in the tone and the timing. Greg felt a hint of disapproval from the math teacher, and that annoyed him.

Greg said, "So you're saying that teachers get paid enough, and that you *don't* want more money, right? And you're saying that you don't want a bigger house with fun stuff all over the place, and more bedrooms and bathrooms? Is that what you're saying?"

Mr. Z smiled. "I'm not saying anything. But I will tell you something that I call the Zenotopoulous Toilet Theory: Most people can only use one bathroom at a time."

After they both laughed a little, the room was quiet for a minute or so.

Then Mr. Z said, "What I was saying earlier, how you should be flattered that Maura tried to copy you? I wasn't kidding. Ever hear the old saying Imitation is the sincerest form of flattery? I think that Maura thinks that you are . . . interesting."

Greg made a face. "No way."

"You know how teachers can tell which boys the sixth-grade girls like?"

Greg shook his head, and he wished Mr. Z would stop talking. He wanted to put his hands over his ears and sing "Yankee Doodle." These were things he did not want to know.

Mr. Z went on. "Girls like the boys that they're always mad at, or shoving, or turning their heads away from, or sticking their tongues out at. Never fails."

From down the hall, Mrs. Davenport called, "Greg? Mrs. Shaw's here. Need any help?"

Greg called back, "No, I'm okay." He jumped up. He wanted to leave before Mr. Z found something else embarrassing to say. Holding the tissues and the cold pack in one hand, Greg got his things together.

Mr. Z said, "Could you leave me a copy of your comic book? I'd like to take a better look at it."

Greg said, "Sure. It's still there on the desk. With Maura's. You can have it. Free." He hurried to the doorway, but then paused and turned back. "Listen, Mr. Z, I'm really sorry about making a mess in your room. Both times."

And Mr. Z said, "Aha—a second apology. Also accepted. That's two for me. One more apology for Maura, and you'll be all caught up."

Greg didn't smile. In his mind he said, *Don't count on it.* Out loud he said, "Well . . . see you tomorrow."

"Yes," said Mr. Z, "and if I'm still on the floor here when you come to class in twenty-two hours, *then* Mrs. Davenport should call an ambulance."

As Greg headed for the front doors, it was Mr. Z who was chuckling.

Chapter 10

SOMETHING FISHY

Greg was quiet in the car on the way home, and so was Maura, but it wasn't awkward. Maura's mom was perfectly happy to do all the talking.

"Oh, you poor *dear*. Let me look at—ooh, such a bruise! And my Maura did this? But it was just an accident . . . and you know that, don't you? That it was an accident? Not like that time in first grade when you bumped Maura off the end of the sliding board. Or that time you threw the snowball into her face. But still . . . you poor *dear*! It must hurt like crazy. Is that compress still cold? . . . Good. Now you just lean back, because we don't want your nose to start bleeding again—not here in the car. Mr. Shaw would give us *all* black eyes if *that* happened—I'm only kidding. But lean back . . . farther . . . that's a good boy. Remember, Maura, when our Tommy got hit with that lacrosse ball? . . . Snapped his nose like a carrot stick, and the *blood*—oh! You would not be*lieve* it! And when I got down to that field . . ."

It was only a five or six-minute drive, but by the time he got home, Greg had heard a detailed description of every major blood-producing event endured by the Shaw family over the past fifteen years.

His own mom was not impressed with his condition. She gave him a quick once-over and said, "Go put that shirt in cold water in the laundry room, then take a shower. Since I'm home a little early, I think I'm going to make lasagna for dinner. How's that sound?" And that was it—from his mom.

By dinnertime the bruise had spread under his left eye, and his big brothers wanted details.

"What do you mean, 'an accident,'" said Ross. "Did you fall off the climbing wall? Or get hit by a baseball? What?"

Greg shook his head. "It was somebody's hand."

Edward said, "Some kid hit you?"

"No," said Greg. "It was just a bump, and she didn't mean to."

"'*She*'?" said Ross. "A *girl* did this? That's lousy. I mean, if a guy whacks you, you can whack him

back, but if it's a girl—"

"Boys." Their dad's tone of voice froze the chatter. "Nobody in this family 'whacks' anybody. It was an accident. So just drop it, all right?"

Ross and Edward let it go—at least until after dinner.

Greg was sitting at his desk doing a tally of the day's sales when both his brothers came bursting into his room. They each had painted on a black eye, and Ross, panting like he'd been running, said, "Hide us, hide us! Me and Edward, we were outside just now, and, and this whole gang of tiny little girls came up and started pounding us! It was terrible! They're everywhere, they're everywhere!" And then they both fell on the floor, howling with laughter.

Greg wanted to laugh too, but he didn't dare. Ross was a high school sophomore and Edward was a freshman. The slightest encouragement of their madness could prove fatal. As coldly as possible, Greg said, "Very funny," and went back to his numbers. He always did the accounting before he started his homework.

About twenty minutes later Greg was almost done with his social studies reading when his mom called up the stairs, "Greg . . . telephone." He trotted out and grabbed the portable phone off the table in the hall.

It was the last person he wanted to hear from.

"Greg, it's me . . . Maura. There was an assignment in math. And you weren't there. So I thought you'd want to know."

Greg said, "Uh, yeah . . . sure. I mean, I was going to call and get it from Ted." And he thought, *What, does she think I'm so stupid that I'd miss a math assignment?* But in a fairly pleasant tone of voice he said, "So, what's the assignment?"

"You have a pencil?"

"Uh-huh." Greg had already hurried back to his room for fear that his brothers might guess he was talking to a girl.

"On page seventeen, it's exercise B," said Maura, "all the even-numbered problems. And I could help, if you don't understand it or something . . . because you weren't there."

"No, that's okay," said Greg. "I can do it. This stuff is still review. So this is good. Yeah . . . this is good."

Maura said, "Mr. Z told everybody to pay

special attention to the decimal points. And he said he might give a quiz. Which means he probably will."

"Good," said Greg. "I mean, that's good to know. Yeah . . . good. This is good."

Already this was the longest phone conversation Greg had ever had with a female who was not his relative, or at least thirty years old, or both. Plus, Greg couldn't help remembering what Mr. Z had said, that he thought Maura found him *interesting*. Even with a topic as safe as a math assignment, Greg felt the strain. He was ready to sign off.

Then Maura said, "I read your comic book again. It makes my unicorn story look just *awful*. I know you said mine isn't a comic book, but I don't really get what that means. Prob'ly because I haven't looked at comic books much. Tommy has some, but I never got into reading them. So I don't really know what makes them so different."

Greg knew what the difference was. It was simple. Because a good comic book is almost like a movie. The words of a comic book are like the script. Every panel is a little scene that moves the story ahead, and time can be speeded up or slowed down, just like in a movie.

And because he understood comics, Greg almost started to explain.

Then he remembered. This was Maura on the phone. Maura the copycat. Maura the idea thief. Maura the enemy.

So Greg said, "Yeah . . . well, listen, I've gotta finish my social studies reading." And since he didn't want to be completely rude, Greg said, "Thanks. For the math assignment."

"You're welcome," Maura said. "Well, see ya round."

Not if I see you first, Greg thought. But he said, "Yup. Bye." And he pushed the phone's Off button.

Sitting there at the desk in his room, Greg knew the *real* reason Maura had called him. It wasn't to try to help him out with his math grade. She had called to fish around for new ideas. She was trying to beat him at his own game. She was trying to get ahead, trying to figure out how to make her dumb little books better so she could make some cash.

And Greg thought, *Nice try, weasel brain. If you think I'm gonna help you make money, think again. You're on your own.*

Chapter 11

NOTES

How come they call it a black eye? Greg stared at his face in the boys' room mirror. It was Friday morning, three minutes before first period, and his black eye was spectacular—just as the nurse had predicted. The deep semicircle was mostly a rich red and purple plum color, rimmed with brownish yellow highlights that arched all the way up to his eyebrow. But there was no black at all.

After the teasing from his big brothers the night before, Greg had gotten on the bus with a good idea of what to expect from the guys at school. But nothing much had happened. Each time the bus stopped, he had moved around, scouting for comic-book customers, and kids had said things like "Nice shiner!" or "Rough night, huh?" Several had asked "How'd *that* happen?"

And that was about all. It was a nice surprise.

But as he left the washroom and made his way to Mrs. Sanborn's class, he had to work up some nerve. He had only two classes today with Maura—math was one, and first-period social studies was the other. He wouldn't get teased in math class—Mr. Z would see to that. But if word had gotten around that Maura had socked him, social studies could be a different story.

Class began, and he could tell some kids were whispering about him. But as Mrs. Sanborn took attendance, Greg was determined not to give it another thought. And anyway, he couldn't afford to. In social studies, daydreaming was danger-ous. The day after each reading assignment, Mrs. Sanborn conducted a rapid-fire question-and-answer session, and class participation counted as one fourth of everyone's grade.

With her teacher's edition of *World Cultures* cradled in her arms, Mrs. Sanborn began pac-ing around the classroom, her words firing twice as fast as her footsteps.

"Mesopotamia is a Greek word that means what—Eileen?"

"Between the rivers."

"Correct. Name one of the rivers—Daniel?"

"The Tigris River."

"Correct. And the other one—Brittany?"

"The Euphrates River."

"Correct. A larger region in the area that includes Mesopotamia—Salina?"

"The Fertile . . . Triangle."

"Half right. The complete correct name of this region—Dennis?"

"The Fertile Crescent."

"Correct. Another river that's in the Fertile Crescent but *not* in Mesopotamia—Greg?"

"The Nile River."

"Correct."

"One of the great ancient cultures associated with the Fertile Crescent—Carl?"

Greg was glad to get called on so early in the Q&A session. He could relax a little now, because there would probably be at least another ten questions before Mrs. Sanborn called on him again.

Like everyone else, Greg had his notebook open on his desk. They were all supposed to be taking notes. But Greg began sketching a picture of Creon riding an animal that looked like the Sphinx. And the face on the Sphinx looked a little like Mrs. Sanborn.

A folded slip of paper dropped onto Greg's desk from behind him. He quickly put his hand over it, but didn't dare turn to see who had thrown it. Mrs. Sanborn had just made a turn and was headed back in his direction.

"The name of the modern nation that includes the largest part of what was called Mesopotamia—Ted?

"Iran."

"Incorrect. Susan—same question."

"Iraq?"

"Correct. In ancient Mesopotamia, what material was most often used for building—Ennis?"

The teacher went past him, and Greg quickly unfolded the paper and held it flat on his notebook. It was a note. Holding his pencil and pretending to write, he read the message.

Greg read it again.

I have to show you something after class.
—Maura

p.s. guess what? I love comics!

He'd seen kids passing notes before. But no one had ever slipped one to him. Sure, it was only from Maura. But she had underlined the word *love* five times. Of course, she was talking about comics. Even so, it was a lot to take in all at once.

"... was the most important use of clay—Greg?"

"Um ... uhh ... writing."

"More specific?"

"Cuneiform writing ... on clay tablets."

"Correct. The rivers in Mesopotamia led to the invention of what important farming practice—Henry?"

It was a near miss. Had Mrs. Sanborn seen the note? Because if she captured it and read it out loud ...

Greg crumpled the slip of paper in his left hand, stuffed it in his pocket, and began taking detailed notes about ancient civilization. But over 80 percent of his mind was worried about current events.

He thought, *Is Maura trying to be, like ... my friend?*

The answer to that seemed a lot like yes.

But why? ... because she loves comic books?

That seemed odd. And sudden.

And if she does *want to be . . . friends?*

There was no clear answer to that one. Greg felt much more comfortable thinking of Maura as a nuisance, or a competitor—or even an enemy.

Mrs. Sanborn's strolling quiz finally ended. During the class discussion that followed, it would have been easy for Greg to turn around and catch Maura's eye, look her in the face, and try to see what she was thinking. But he kept taking careful notes.

And when Mrs. Sanborn let them begin their reading assignment, he could have turned and pretended to borrow something from Maura. Instead he opened his textbook. He pumped paragraph after paragraph of dusty history into his mind, trying to dry up his curiosity.

Greg's concentration slipped, and he remembered again what Mr. Z had said about Maura. He tried to forget all that, tried to remember his great publishing plans, tried to think about his sales figures for the week, about how he wanted to sell a hundred units, about how he had to make his goal.

But the end of first period was coming, tick

by tock. And then he'd have to walk out into the wide-open hallway. Maura had already warned him: *I have to show you something.* She was going to track him down, and there was nothing he could do about it.

So as Mrs. Sanborn dismissed the class, Greg decided all he could do was just walk out the door, head for gym class, and let the future come. And try not to get another black eye.

Chapter 12

A LOOK

Maura cornered him before he got ten feet from Mrs. Sanborn's door.

"Greg! Look what I got last night. After we talked. From the library."

Greg was relieved. It was just a big book. Maura had it out of her backpack, and she pushed it into his hands. She was excited. "It's called *Understanding Comics*, and it's great, and I read the whole thing last night, and I think I get it. Comics, I mean. How they work. And look at this." She handed him two pieces of paper.

There were drawings on the sheets. Right away Greg knew what he was seeing. It was the rescue scene from Maura's mini–picture book, *The Lost Unicorn*. First there was a close-up of the unicorn's head, with its teeth showing and nostrils snorting, and a reflection of the ogre's tower in its large, dark eye. Then

there was a wide view of the creature with its
head lowered as it charged the tree next to the
tower, and then another close-up as its horn bit
into the rough wood—complete with a spiky
sound balloon. Maura had drawn the face of
the princess in the tower window as the unicorn struck the tree; the tree falling against the
tower; the branches cracking, leaves flying; the

slippered foot of the princess on a branch of the tree; the princess pressing her face against the neck of the unicorn; and then the princess on the back of the rearing animal, with a final close-up of her hand twined into the hair of the unicorn's mane.

Maura had turned two picture-book pages into ten panels—comic-book panels.

Greg was speechless, blown away. The sizing of the panels, the sequence of the pictures—Maura got it. She understood how a comic worked. These were just pencil sketches, and the scale wasn't always perfect, but the drawings were still so strong, so powerful. With a little work, and if they were inked and shaded just right, they would be fabulous, they would be . . . dangerous.

Maura was watching his face. "What d'you think? Are they any good?"

Greg tried to keep his face blank as his mind raced ahead.

If he told her how great these were, it would be like unchaining a monster that was going to turn around and eat him alive. Because if Maura could make drawings like these, she could make *fantastic* comic books. And selling her comics? That would be easy—*too* easy. She'd get rich in no time. Maura was plenty smart. It wouldn't take her long to figure out how to make copies, and how to fold and trim the pages. And here she was, standing in front of him, and she wanted him to approve, maybe even help her, give her some advice.

Greg kept his eyes on the paper. Knowing that Maura was looking at his face, watching for clues, he frowned. Then he slowly shook his head, and got ready to tell a lie. He looked up from the drawings. He was going to tell her these drawings were pretty bad, tell her she'd better stick with her little picture books, maybe tell her to give up drawing completely— and that she should *definitely* forget about the comics business.

All this took only a second to spin through Greg's mind. He looked Maura in the eye, gave her a sad, understanding smile, and he said— But he didn't. Because Brittany Paxton and Eileen Ripley rushed up next to Maura, and Brittany said, "Oooh, this is so *sweet*! First Maura and Greg have a big quarrel yesterday in math, then Maura throws Greg a little *note* in social studies, and now Greg and Maura are all lovey-dovey out in the hall." Turning to Eileen, she said, "What sounds better, 'Greg and Maura' or 'Maura and Greg'? I think 'Maura and Greg.' It's *per*fect, don't you think?"

And then came a flood of giggles.

A more experienced guy would have simply turned away and gone on about his business. But Greg panicked. No one, not even his notorious big brothers, had ever suggested he liked a girl, or that a girl might like him.

Except for the area around his left eye, Greg's whole face turned deep pink. "Don't be stupid!" he snarled. "I can't help it if somebody throws paper at my desk, and I can't help it if she sticks some dopey pictures in my face either. Here—take this junk." He shoved the sketches and the book into Maura's hands and said, "Get away from me!"

Eileen said, "Oooh—so *tough*—we better call him Big Greg . . . Big Greg and Maura."

More giggles.

But by then Big Greg was gone, hurrying to his next class, trying to put some distance between himself and that whole scene.

And he succeeded. The gym was all the way

at the other end of the school, and the second Greg got there he grabbed a basketball and challenged John Elders to a quick game of one-on-one. In two minutes he was breathing hard and sweating. He was losing, too, but that didn't matter.

What mattered was that he had gotten away from those girls—all of them. Away from what Eileen and Brittany said, and away from their laughter.

But what Greg could not get away from was the wounded look on Maura's face as he had shoved those pictures into her hands.

As he charged in for a layup, he thought, *I didn't ask her to show that stuff to me. If she likes her pictures, she can go ahead and try to do something with them. It's got nothing to do with me. Like she said, it's a free country.* And as he spun around and scrambled for his own rebound, he thought, *I don't owe her one thing. What's she ever done for me? . . . except steal my ideas and bother me every chance she gets.*

But after saying all this to himself, Greg could still see that look on Maura's face.

Chapter 13

LOCKOUT

By the middle of third period Greg had put the whole incident with Maura and Eileen and Brittany out of his mind. Gym class had helped. They'd had a great soccer game out on the big field, and he'd been the left forward—good for two goals. Plus he'd sold seven more copies of his comic book. And now the whole language arts class was having a big argument about which was better—*Holes*, the book, or *Holes*, the movie. Life was back to normal.

Then the intercom speaker next to the clock on the wall crackled to life. It was Mrs. Ogden, the school secretary. "Mrs. Lindahl?"

The teacher held up her hand for quiet. "Yes?" All eyes swung to the speaker, as if there was something to see.

"Pardon the interruption. Will you please send Gregory Kenton to the office?"

Mrs. Lindahl nodded at the speaker and said, "He'll be right there." Then she nodded at Greg.

When the secretary said his name, Greg had felt his stomach tighten, felt a tingle in his mouth and across the top of his scalp. But he pushed back the fear, stood up, and walked out the door into the hallway.

The hall was empty, quiet. His cross-trainers squeaked on the tiles as he walked. Greg told himself, *Could be a message from my mom. Like maybe a dentist appointment after school. So I don't take the bus home.*

But Greg knew he was kidding himself. This had to be about something else. And when he turned the last corner and looked through the office windows, he knew. Maura was sitting on the little wooden bench on one side of the principal's door. And Mr. Z sat in the chair on the other side. So this was going to be about what had happened yesterday, about arguing and yelling in math class, about getting whacked in the nose. Because fighting of any kind was absolutely forbidden at Ashworth Intermediate, a huge no-no, right up there with vandalism and stealing. And

Mrs. Davenport came down hard on fighting. Always.

When Greg entered the office, Mrs. Ogden looked up and then pointed to the bench. Greg sat down.

Without turning her head, Maura whispered, "This is *your* fault. I have *never* been called to the principal's office before."

Greg snorted and whispered back, "Well, boohoo. We didn't even fight. It was an accident. We can prove it. So relax. We're just gonna get yelled at a little."

"Or *suspended*," Maura said.

The principal's door opened. "Mr. Zenotopoulous, Maura, Greg—please come in. Sit down."

She pointed, and Greg and Maura took the chairs in front of her desk, and Mr. Z sat off to the right a few feet.

Mrs. Davenport sat down. "I've talked now with Mr. Z and also with the school nurse about what happened yesterday. I understand that Greg's knock on the nose was an accident, and I'm ready to let it go at that. But I want both of you to know how serious I am about fighting. I will have none of that in this school—and I'm not going to have angry shouting or arguments either, because that's almost the same thing. You two have a bad habit of not getting along. You both need to grow out of that, but until that happens, my advice—no, my *direction*—is that you simply keep away from each other. And to help this happen, Greg, starting Monday, you will have Mr. Scully for first-period social studies, and Maura, at sixth period on Monday you will report to Mrs. Toroni's level-four math class. Any questions?"

Maura shook her head. Her face was pale. She wasn't going to say a thing. She felt lucky not to be suspended. Or expelled. After all, she was the one who had thrown that wicked right hook.

Greg also shook his head. The new schedule was fine with him. In fact, it was great. The less he saw of Maura, the better.

Mrs. Davenport looked from face to face, and said, "All right, then. That's that."

Greg put his hands on the arms of his chair, all set to stand up and leave.

"Now about *this* situation," the principal said, and she opened a folder. She held up a

copy of *Return of the Hunter* in one hand, and a copy of *The Lost Unicorn* in the other. "I saw these in Mr. Z's room yesterday afternoon, and he tells me that you two have been selling these little books around the school. Is that correct? I've been seeing them all over, especially this one." She shook the Creon comic.

Talking fast, Maura pointed at the unicorn book and said, "I only made five of mine, and I mostly gave them to my friends. I just sold one."

Mrs. Davenport said, "Greg, what about you?"

He nodded at her other hand. "I've been selling that one since Monday. And everybody really likes it. So I'm working on a whole series. Did you read it?"

Mrs. Davenport seemed surprised, both by Greg's chatty reply, and by his question. She gave a halting nod, and Greg said, "Did you like the story?"

The principal put a stern look on her face and said, "We're not discussing the quality of your writing today. Do you remember the talk we had right here in my office last June? I told you I did *not* want you selling things at school. Do you remember that?"

Greg had an answer to her question. But he didn't just speak up. Instead he raised his hand. He was about to tell the principal she was wrong, so it seemed like a good idea to wait politely for her permission to speak.

When she nodded at him, Greg said, "Last June I was selling little toys. And you told me that I wasn't allowed to sell them at school. So I stopped right away, just like you said. And I'm not selling toys. I'm selling books."

A student telling a principal she's mistaken— that doesn't happen very often. And there's a good reason for that.

Mrs. Davenport's eyes flashed, and with clipped words she said, "I know perfectly well what you are selling. *This* is a comic book, and in my view, comic books are practically toys, and *bad* toys at that. This is hardly what I would call a book. When I saw the first one of these on Monday, and I saw your name on it, I should have called you in here that instant and put a stop to it. Because look what's happening now."

Mrs. Davenport opened the folder again and picked up four or five other little handmade comic books. She fanned them out like playing cards and held them up for all to see. Greg could only see parts of the covers, but what he saw didn't look good. The artwork was crude and poorly drawn. One cover showed an evil-looking muscleman holding a big knife, and the title was *Just in Time to Die.* Another one was titled *Crundoon,* and it showed a huge slobbering monster biting off the top of a girl's head.

After a pause to let the pictures sink in, the principal said, "Because of your example, everybody now seems to think that they can make nasty, violent stuff like this, and then bring it to school, and sell it."

Greg put his hand up again, and this time he started speaking before the principal nodded at him. "But my comic's not like that. I mean, there's action in the story, and things get sort of rough, but I wasn't trying to make it violent. It's history. I based it on real Stone Age people—I got books from the library."

Mrs. Davenport waved her hand. "I'm not going to have a discussion about which comic book is worse than another. I am going to say what I said to you last June, and this time let me be even clearer. Do *not* sell things at school. Do not sell *anything*. School is a place for learning and thinking. It is not a place for buying and selling. Mr. Zenotopoulous, do you have anything to add?"

The question caught Mr. Z off guard. "Um . . . well, I was just going to say that . . . that I think it's important—what you've said to Greg and Maura. And . . . and that's all."

Mrs. Davenport stood up, and as if there were strings connecting everyone, the other three people popped up too. "Very well then," the principal said. "We all understand one another. And I'll be making an all-school announcement during sixth-grade lunch today so that everyone else understands too. Now, let's all get back to work—our *real* work. This is a school day."

And with that, the meeting ended.

In the hall outside the office, Maura turned right and hurried toward the science rooms. Since his language arts class was in room 25, Greg turned left and walked alongside Mr. Z. Neither of them spoke.

About halfway down the long hall, Greg wanted to ask Mr. Z a question. He held back, because the question seemed improper, too bold. But . . . hadn't they both been knocked flat on their backs together, down onto the bloody math-room floor? And hadn't they discussed money and careers and the Zenotopoulous Toilet Theory? Didn't sharing that experience mean they were sort of related now—not exactly blood brothers, but . . . *something*, right?

And so, relying on this odd feeling of kinship, and hoping that Mr. Z wouldn't get offended, Greg worked up the nerve to ask his question. "Mr. Z? I was wondering . . . do you really agree with Mrs. Davenport, with everything she said?"

Mr. Z hesitated half a second, and then nodding his head, he said, "Mrs. Davenport is very logical. Kids can't be scrounging around all day trying to make money at school. It's not the right place for that."

"But what she said about comic books?" Greg asked. "And *my* comic book? Do *you* think my comic book is 'nasty'? And 'violent'?"

It took six steps along the hallway before Mr. Z had an answer to that one, almost to the door of room 25. "Personally, I have nothing against comic books. And as a comic book, I didn't mind yours at all. It's actually quite good. But as something to sell at school, no. Mrs. Davenport's right about that part."

Greg went back to his desk in language arts class feeling a little better. At least Mr. Z wasn't lumping Creon in with those other comics. But the facts were still pretty discouraging. He wasn't going to be able to sell his comics at school. Sure, he could still write stories, still do his drawings, and still make all the comics he wanted to. And he could even try to sell them to kids some other way. But it would be so much harder. There didn't seem much point to it. School was where the kids were, and the kids were his readers, his customers.

And it had to happen just when things were going so well, too. Fourteen more units, and he would have made his goal for the first week—one hundred comics sold.

It felt like another punch in the nose.

Chapter 14

SEVENTY-FIVE PERCENT OF NOTHING

No lunch recess. It was the only thing Greg really hated about sixth grade. After the kids finished eating, they had to dump their trays, sit back down, and wait for the bell. No walking around, no loud talking, and Mr. Percy, the custodian, was always there, leaning on his mop handle, watching.

It reminded Greg of mealtime in an old prison movie. Mr. Percy was like the guard, always edgy until the prisoners were locked up in their cells again. Except the convicts got to go out into the exercise yard every afternoon, and the sixth graders didn't.

Greg had done some thinking since third period, and he'd decided he ought to say something to Maura about her drawings. He hadn't actually lied to her in the hallway after social studies, but he had come close. And he remembered that hurt look she gave him as he'd shoved her pictures back in her face.

Yes, Maura was annoying, and she was a copy-cat, and he was glad Mrs. Davenport had fixed it so he was going to see even less of her every day. Still, she had gone out of her way to ask his opinion about her drawings, and her excitement about comic books seemed real. So why not tell her the truth about her artwork? It was the least he could do. And besides, it wouldn't cost him anything now that he couldn't sell comics at school.

Greg knew that if he went over and tried to talk to Maura at her table, he'd be surrounded by girls. No way could he say what he wanted to with an audience like that. Plus, with Mrs. Davenport's orders to keep away from Maura, he didn't dare just walk up to her.

So he ate fast and watched carefully. And when Maura got up to take her tray to the drop-off window, Greg made his move. His timing had to be perfect. It was, but Maura saw him coming.

As Greg slipped into the short line behind her, he saw her shoulders stiffen. So he talked fast, his voice low. "That thing in the office went okay, don't you think? I mean, it stinks

not being able to sell comics anymore. But at least we didn't get in trouble. Not even a detention. Pretty good, huh?"

Maura didn't turn, didn't nod, didn't react. Nothing.

So Greg took a deep breath and said, "Listen, I didn't mean what I said. After social studies. When Eileen and Brittany came up. But you heard what they said. And it just—"

"Just *what*?" Maura hissed, still keeping her back to him. "Did the big, mean girls *scare* you? You could've said something like, 'We're just talking,' you know. Because you only made everything look worse, which is just what they wanted. Besides, who's stupid enough to even *care* what those two think? Oh . . . I forgot— *you* are!"

If Maura wanted to trade insults, she was messing with the wrong guy. "Oh yeah?" Greg said. "Well, *you're*—"

"I'm what?" Maura whipped around so fast that the empty milk carton flew off her tray.

Greg had the words. He could have hit her hard. But that wasn't what he wanted. He took a breath.

Again Maura demanded, "I'm *what?*"

"You're . . . you're right," Greg said. "What I did was stupid. And what I said was stupid. So . . . I'm sorry."

Then he bent down, picked up her milk carton, and tossed it into the recycling barrel along with his own.

"Oh . . . ," Maura said. She was surprised he'd apologized, and also that he'd picked up her trash. She said, "Um . . . thanks," and then slid her tray onto the conveyor belt.

Greg said, "You're welcome," and then he dumped his tray too.

With his hands empty, Greg felt suddenly awkward. He missed having his red pencil case to hang on to. He stuffed his hands into his pockets. He said, "So . . . don't you want to know what I was thinking this morning?

About your drawings? Before . . . all that?"

Maura said, "Yeah . . . but only if you were going to say something good." And she turned and walked toward the crowd of kids at the dessert table.

Greg followed her, glad that the noise and talking in the cafeteria seemed to be getting a little louder. The sound was like camouflage. He edged up next to Maura and said, "If you only want to know what was good, your drawing won't ever get better."

She turned her head. "So some of it was good? Really?"

Greg looked into her face to see if she was kidding. Her eyes didn't lie. Maura actually had no idea how brilliant her pictures were. And it struck him that this might be the first time he had ever looked into Maura's face when they hadn't been yelling at each other.

He turned his face forward, and took a step closer to the dessert table. Choosing his words carefully, he said, "I don't want you to get all conceited or anything, because your pictures . . . well, they're good. Maybe it's just beginner's luck or something. But I don't think so. Because . . . you got it—the whole idea of how pictures work in a comic. The timing of the panels in that scene? You just . . . nailed it."

Greg sneaked a sideways look at Maura. Her cheek, usually pale next to her blond hair, was flushed with color. She was smiling slightly— trying not to, but smiling.

He said, "There's more. Ready?"

Maura angled her head his way, but wouldn't look him in the face. She nodded.

He said, "Okay. Some problems. You know what scale is? In a drawing?"

Maura nodded, and Greg said, "So tell me."

She said, "It's when you make sure things look like they're the right size compared to other things. Like, if a unicorn looks like it's actually bigger than a tree, then the scale is messed up."

Greg said, "Right. So, in a couple of your panels, the scale was wrong. But only in a few. The truth is, they're amazing. Just . . . incredible."

With something in her voice that sounded like fear, Maura said, "You're not . . . just saying this, right?"

Greg shook his head and said, "No." Then he said, "I mean, I'm not some big expert or anything. But I've seen a lot of comics, and I think your pictures are really good. Really."

Without even looking Maura in the face, he could tell how much those few words meant to her. And it seemed like she actually cared about his opinion. It was scary to feel how much power that gave him. And suddenly Greg felt kind of responsible—like he wanted to help her. It was an entirely new feeling.

But Greg didn't let himself get carried away. His business mind kicked in, and in a flash he saw a way to be sort of helpful, and also to possibly make a little money.

"So," he said, "how'd you like to make your whole unicorn story over into a comic book? And then print some copies? And then try to sell them—not at school, but there are other places. If you want, I could help. And your comic could be one of the Chunky Comics. And if any of them sell, then you could even make some money, share in the profits. And if you come up with more story ideas, you could make more. And try to sell them. What d'you think?"

It seemed like a decent idea to Greg. And a very generous offer.

Without missing a beat, Maura said, "How much money would I get?"

"Forty percent of the profits on every copy sold—just on your comics, not mine," Greg added, again feeling generous.

Maura shook her head. "Seventy-five percent. For my own comics. And you don't get to tell me what my stories should be about or anything."

They both took a step closer to the dessert table.

"Fifty percent," said Greg. And he thought, *She is the bossiest, most annoying, most—*

"Seventy-five percent," Maura said, "or else I'll just go ahead and figure out how to do it all myself."

Everything he did not like about Maura came crashing back into his mind, and Greg was tempted to shout, *Fine, go ahead and do it all yourself, you stupid, stubborn lump!* But he wasn't going to give her the satisfaction of seeing him get angry. Besides, they weren't going to sell many comics now, maybe none at all. And seventy-five percent of nothing . . . is nothing. So Greg said, "Deal. Seventy-five percent. But, you have to buy me an ice-cream sandwich. Right now."

Maura stepped up, laid four quarters on the dessert table, reached into the freezer, grabbed two ice-cream sandwiches, and slapped one of them into Greg's hand. She looked him in the eye, cracked half a smile, and said, "Deal."

Three minutes later as Greg sat at his regular table enjoying the last gooey bites of his free ice-cream sandwich, the speakers crackled, and the PA chimes sounded. Silence settled over the cafeteria as Mrs. Davenport began to speak. Again Greg thought of a prison movie. It was time for a few words from the warden.

"Good afternoon, boys and girls, and good afternoon also to all the teachers and staff. I'm sorry to interrupt classes this way, but I have an important all-school announcement.

"Some of our students have been making small comic books and bringing them to school. I have looked at some of these, and they are not the sort of thing we want here at Ashworth Intermediate School. Also, I have learned that some students have been selling these little comic books to their friends right here at school.

"Even if these comics were appropriate—and they are not—even then, no one would ever be permitted to sell them at school. Our town School Committee has a strict policy about this.

"So please listen carefully: Starting right now, I want all students and all teachers to understand that these little comic books may not be *brought* to school, they may not be *created* at school, and they certainly may not be *sold* at school.

"Thank you all for your cooperation, and have a productive afternoon."

The chocolate wafers were Greg's favorite part of an ice-cream sandwich, and as he chewed the last sticky bits from his left thumb, he thought, *So that's it. The warden has spoken. Chunky Comics is now officially dead.*

And suddenly Greg was surprised, startled, almost shocked. Not that Chunky Comics was dead. He'd known that was going to happen. What amazed him was that he wasn't more upset about it. Because only yesterday he'd been shouting in Maura's face, all set to go Cro-Magnon on her because she was cutting into his profits. And today his whole comic-book empire was crushed, all that money was swirling down the drain, and what was he doing about it? Eating ice cream.

And Greg thought, *What's _wrong_ with me? I should be furious; I should be pounding on this table, shouting, "Unfair, unfair, unfair!"*

But Greg didn't have a chance to think more deeply about this. Because at that moment the bell rang. Everyone stood up, Mr. Percy began barking orders, and the inmates at the Ashworth Intermediate Security Facility started trudging back to their cells.

After math class on Friday afternoon, Greg rushed out and went straight to the art room. He needed every possible minute to work on his wire sculpture. Maura took her time leaving room 27, and as she got to the door, Mr. Z called, "Maura? Just a quick word, please."

She turned around, made her way through the other kids, and walked over to stand in front of his desk.

Mr. Z started slowly. "I just wanted to say that I feel like what happened yesterday between you and Greg was partly my fault. When Greg started yelling, I should have pulled him right out into the hall. Then all that mess wouldn't have happened, and you wouldn't have been called to the principal's office today. Or been switched out of my class—and by the way, that was not my idea. So I wanted to say I'm sorry. And I feel like I've turned you two into worse enemies than ever."

Maura shook her head and said, "It's okay. Really. Things are better now. I mean, it's not like Greg and I are friends or anything, but we're sort of in business. We've got a deal and everything. I'm going to make comic books. For Greg's company."

Mr. Z's dark eyebrows went up. "Greg's company? Well, that's . . . good news. Great." He smiled, and didn't seem to know what to say next.

"So . . . ," Maura said, "can I go now? I can't be late for language arts. Again."

"Of course." Mr. Z nodded. "Go right ahead. And . . . and have a good weekend."

"You too, Mr. Z."

After Maura was already out the door, Mr. Z called, "And if you two want any advice, I know some economics. And accounting . . . business stuff."

Maura called back, "Thanks."

Earlier, during lunchtime, Maura Shaw had listened to the announcement from the principal, and she had heard the same words Greg had heard. But for her, Chunky Comics wasn't dead—it was just coming to life. She intended to make Greg keep his word. He was going to help her turn *The Lost Unicorn* into a real comic book—whether he actually wanted to or not.

And Maura couldn't wait to get started.

Chapter 15

LESSONS

Friday night at the Kenton house was family movie time, but tonight Ross and Edward had gone out with their high-school friends, which was fine with Greg. That meant *he* got to pick the movie. By seven thirty Greg had his mom and dad, half the couch, a big bowl of popcorn, a bottle of root beer, and good old Indiana Jones all to himself.

The movie started with a bang. Between the action and the music and the sound effects, Greg barely noticed the doorbell, barely noticed his mom getting up to answer it. She came back to the family room and said, "Greg, it's Maura Shaw."

With his eyes still on the screen, Greg said, "What?"

She said, "Put the movie on Pause." When the room was quiet, she said, "It's Maura Shaw. At the door."

"Maura?" Greg said. "What's she want?"

His mom shrugged. "She just asked if you were home."

Greg took a quick sip of root beer and got up off the couch.

Maura stood by the door. She held a big brown mailing envelope, and before Greg could say a word, she handed it to him. "New drawings. I did them after school. And you have to look at them before I make any more—to tell me how I'm doing. I know I've got the size right, because they're just like the ones in your Creon story. And I used good art paper. Because I know you have to put ink on them. But you have to tell me about everything else."

Did Maura ask, "Is this a bad time?" No. Did she say, "I'll leave these so you can look at them"? No. She stood there, tapping her foot, bossy as ever. Greg hated cold popcorn, and he wished he'd kept his mouth shut about Maura's pictures.

He ripped open the envelope and yanked out the papers so he could whip through them. Then he could push this intruder out the door and get back to his movie. But Maura's first picture grabbed him and pulled him in.

She had done the cover art. The picture focused on the unicorn, its long, twisted horn poking all the way up through the word *Unicorn* in the title—a nice touch. But best of all, Maura had drawn dark woods with the scary outline of bare trees, and in the distance, the tower. And in the bottom right corner of the picture, an ogre lurked in the undergrowth, eyes huge, jaws open.

Greg nodded. "*Great* cover. Really. This is

great." Without thinking, he sat down cross-legged on the front-hall carpet and flipped to the next picture, which was page one, where the unicorn first realizes she's lost. The small page was split in half from the upper right corner to the lower left corner, which made two panels shaped like triangles. The top panel showed the frightened creature walking down a forest path, looking back over her shoulder. The dividing line was a jagged lightning bolt, and below it there was a close-up of the unicorn's eyes looking up at storm clouds, with the woods and the darkness crowding in.

Still nodding, Greg looked at the third drawing and said, "This is good too." Maura had already figured out how to use every bit of space—a big challenge on such tiny pages. One larger panel helped the reader understand the whole scene, and other smaller ones zoomed in on the most dramatic details. She had also trimmed the story down into a real comic-book script. The words were penciled into the speech balloons.

"Greg?" It was his dad. "Should we hold the movie?"

"Um . . . no, it's okay," Greg called back. "I've

seen it. And I have to help on this a little. . . . It's some drawings. We'll be down in the playroom. I'll be there later."

At the moment Maura's sketches were a lot more interesting than the Temple of Doom. Greg wanted to try inking one or two of them.

"Here." He handed all the drawings back to Maura and pointed her toward the basement doorway. "Go down there. I've got to get some stuff from my room."

Three minutes later Greg carried a bin of his art materials into the playroom. He dragged a chair over and set up a work area on the Ping-Pong table. He took Maura's cover picture out of the envelope, hurried upstairs to the family room, ignored his mom and dad and the movie, and made two copies of the cover—practice sheets. Greg trotted back to the playroom, sat down, chose a small brush, dipped it into a bottle of india ink, and began to experiment. The unicorn was going to be white, so that meant he had to darken everything around it. He loved working with the sharp contrast of black and white. He put down the brush, picked up a pen, and dipped its thin metal point into the ink. Time to add some

detail to the unicorn's mane.

Maura came and stood behind him, craning her neck to see. Greg ignored her. She moved to his right side, put a hand on the Ping-Pong table, and leaned in closer. "Hey!" Greg said. "Don't shake the table!"

"Well, what am I supposed to do?" she asked.

"Do whatever you want. Watch TV. Go home. But don't shake the table. Here, take this paper. And a ruler. And there are pencils and erasers in the bin. Make some more drawings. You can sit over there."

Maura set up a little work space on the low table in front of the TV. She sat on the floor with her back against the couch, facing Greg. She shuffled through her envelope of papers. She got out her story script and found the next page she wanted to work on. She used the ruler to draw the boundaries for the page. Then she made a few marks on the paper. She looked at them, and then erased them all. She made another start, but then stopped and rubbed it all out again. She couldn't get into it. And she knew why: Sitting on the floor in Greg Kenton's playroom was just too weird.

Maura got up quietly and tiptoed over next to the Ping-Pong table. She stood at Greg's elbow, watching him add tiny lines with a crow-quill pen. When it looked like a good moment to speak, she said, "I forgot to tell you. I really want to do all the lettering myself."

Greg looked up at her and made a face. "Well . . . it can't be in cursive, like you used before. It's too hard to read, especially when it's small. How's your printing?"

"Are you kidding?" said Maura. "Mrs. Layton, in third grade? She had to *force* me to use cursive. I was *so* good at printing."

Greg reached for a lettering pen, the kind with a point that's almost like a needle. He unscrewed the cap and slid a piece of lined paper toward Maura. "Here. This is the kind of pen you have to use. Don't push hard, or you'll wreck it. Try writing something."

Maura made a few marks to get the feel of

the pen point, and then she wrote,

This pen is different, but I like it.

Greg looked at the sentence and nodded. "Pretty good."

It was actually neater and clearer than his own lettering, and he'd been working on his for two years. He said, "But you'll have to practice and get it a little smaller, and you have to keep watching how many words you use—the fewer the better."

"I know that," said Maura.

"Oh, so now you're an expert, right?"

"No," snapped Maura, "but I'm not dumb. I really do get it, how the pictures have to tell most of the story. So don't talk to me like I'm an idiot."

Greg bit back a perfect insult. He pointed at the other table and said, "So go be a genius over there, okay? I'm trying to get something done here."

For the next thirty minutes there was no talking—only the soft scratching sounds of pens or pencils on paper.

Greg's mom came to ask if they wanted something to eat, but she stopped halfway down the stairs, and then crept back up. She didn't want to interrupt. Because what she saw reminded her of two kindergartners at the art tables, each child bent over some work, each completely unaware of the other.

Which wasn't quite true.

Yes, Maura was working on a new minipage, and she was in that quiet, creative zone in her mind. But in the back of her thinking, she wished she could just walk over and stand behind Greg, watch him lay down those clear brush strokes and impossibly thin lines of ink. The kid was creative. Smart, too. And almost nice sometimes, like when he'd apologized in the lunchroom earlier in the day. And even when he was acting all tough and mean, he was still funny, like when he'd made her buy that ice-cream sandwich as part of the deal. Maura had to admit it: Sometimes Greg was actually sort of cute.

And Greg hadn't forgotten that Maura was sitting ten feet away. He glanced up at her every few minutes, just a flick of his eyes, as if to make sure she was still there. Her talent was amazing, and she seemed willing to try anything. Of course, any minute now, she would probably go nuts again, and do something that would make him want to strangle her. But when she wasn't trying to rule the world, like when she kept her big mouth shut and just sat there wrinkling her nose at a drawing, Maura wasn't that bad to have around. And think of it—a girl who loved comics. How cool was that?

Almost an hour later Greg broke the silence. "There. Two pages and the cover, all inked. You get anything done?"

Maura nodded and stood up stiffly. "Two more pages." She walked over and laid them on the Ping-Pong table.

Greg stood up and pulled Maura's new penciled pages closer. And he reached over and spread out his finished inking work in front of Maura. Then both of them leaned over the table, each inspecting the other's work. They were both impressed with what they saw, but there wasn't any gushing.

"Yeah, those are okay," Greg said.

Maura nodded. "Yours too."

The phone rang, and Maura said, "Bet you anything that's my mom."

It was, and Maura had to leave.

"Here," Greg said. "Take these home and do the lettering. You can borrow my pen."

Maura nodded, and Greg sat down and went back to work.

She said, "I'm going to bring over more pictures tomorrow."

Greg shrugged. "Whatever." Then he thought a second and said, "But don't come until about two." He had promised to wash both of the Jansens' cars before noon, and he had Saturday chores around home, too. Plus, both his brothers might be gone by two in the afternoon. They were always worth avoiding.

Maura gathered her things together and left. Greg didn't walk up to the front door with her, didn't even say good-bye. He was too busy.

Greg stayed at the Ping-Pong table almost another hour, and before he went up to say good night to his mom and dad, he had finished inking two more pages.

As he lay in bed looking at the patterns that the streetlight and tree branches made on his ceiling, Greg thought about the evening. Inking Maura's drawings had been so different from working on his own pictures. He felt like he'd had to be more careful with hers—careful not to put too many of his own ideas into them, careful not to change her drawing style. And he had to admit it: The results were good.

But as he drifted toward the edge of sleep, there was something else he would not admit. Admitting this other thing would have been too dangerous. Because what Greg wouldn't admit was that he was almost sort of a little bit maybe halfway glad about Maura. Coming back. To work on her comic again. On Saturday. At two.

Chapter 16

ART AND MONEY

Greg started watching for Maura a little before two on Saturday, and when she arrived ten minutes later, he opened the front door before she could ring the bell. Edward was gone for the afternoon, but Ross was upstairs. He had done his morning chores and gone back to bed. It was always best to let sleeping big brothers stay that way. There'd be a lot less chance of getting teased about having a girl visit. Not that there was anything to tease about. Maura had only come over to work.

She had already finished the lettering on the cover and the two pages Greg had inked before she left Friday night. And she had also done the pencil sketches for all but three pages of the rest of the comic.

Maura followed Greg down the steps to the playroom. They went and sat in their places. Greg dipped his brush, Maura sharpened her pencils, and they both got right to work. It was all business. There was no chat, barely a word between them for almost two hours.

The inking work went well, and by four thirty Greg had five more pages ready to letter. Maura had finished her last three drawings, and then she'd started in on more lettering. Greg was amazed at how much faster the work went when he didn't have to do every step by himself. The playroom was like a little comic-book factory.

Maura left a little after five because she had to go out to dinner with her family, but she took all the inked pages with her, and promised to bring them back Sunday afternoon with the lettering done.

It wasn't much fun to sit alone at the Ping-Pong table and grind out the pages, but Greg went to the basement again after dinner. He stayed on the job until he'd finished another three pages, and then he gave himself the rest of the night off to watch some TV.

Maura came over after lunch on Sunday, and she was pleased with herself. "See? I finished lettering all the pages you inked yesterday."

"Except for these three I finished last night,"

Greg said. "So get back to work, you slacker."

"Very funny." Maura sat down, and so did Greg. Unscrewing the cap of the lettering pen, she said, "I bet I'll be done with my job before you're done with yours."

Greg snorted. "Bet you won't."

"How much?" said Maura.

"One ice-cream sandwich."

Maura grinned. "You're on!" And they both bent over their work.

But two minutes later Maura looked up suddenly and said, "Hey! No fair—I *can't* finish first. I can't letter until *after* you ink!"

Greg nodded and smiled. "And you figured that out all by yourself? Good work. Just be glad I didn't bet you twenty dollars."

It was almost three o'clock when Greg handed Maura the last inked page for lettering. It was the back cover of the comic, which was designed like a picture frame with information in the middle. Fifteen minutes later the words were all in place.

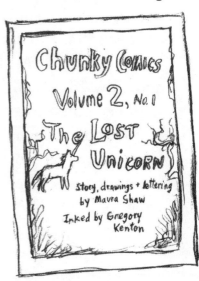

153

"Okay, now we trim each drawing to the exact size of the pages of the finished comic book." Greg pulled two pairs of scissors out of his materials bin and handed one to Maura. "Trim along the pencil lines. And be careful."

Ten minutes later there were sixteen small pages laid out in order on the Ping-Pong table, front cover to back cover.

"Now we've got to paste every piece of art into its right place on two master copy sheets—eight pages per sheet. I just use a glue stick. And the pages that look upside down and out of order, that all changes when you fold the printed sheet at the end."

Maura nodded, her eyes bright as she took in each step of the process.

When both master copy sheets were pasted up, Greg said, "Time for the copier—and bring your scissors." Maura followed him upstairs.

Once again Greg had hoped that both Ross and Edward would be absent. Only half his wish had come true. Ross was sprawled on the family-room couch, half asleep in front of a Clint Eastwood movie. A can of ginger ale and an empty bag of pretzels sat on the table in front of him. He opened one eye and saw

Maura, then looked at Greg and winked. "Hey, little buddy . . . I see your *lady*friend is here."

Greg felt the urge to lash out, like he'd done with Eileen and Brittany at school on Friday morning. But this time he didn't take the bait. He said, "We're just copying some artwork. For a project we're doing. And it's gonna make noise. We have to."

Ross heaved himself up off the couch, shut off the TV, burped, mumbled, "'Scuse me" in Maura's general direction, and went looking for a quieter place to waste another hour or two.

Greg said, "I got this paper that's good and bright, but it's not as thick as regular copy paper. Makes it easier to fold."

After placing the first master sheet face down on the glass, he pushed Print, and then held up the copy for Maura to see. Pointing at a gray area, he said, "See that? I can change the settings and make that part darker. It ought to be solid black. Except for that, it's a good copy." The machine beeped as Greg made the change, and then he pushed the Print button.

Again he held up the copy. "Look okay to you?"

Maura nodded.

"Good," said Greg. "Then let's print another fourteen." The machine began whirring away. He said, "This'll take a few minutes. Want something to eat? Or drink?"

Maura shook her head, watching the pages come out of the printer, one by one.

When the copies were done, Greg said, "This next part is tricky. We have to take the first master copy off the copier, and put on the second one . . . like this. And make sure it's facing the right way. I had a *lot* of trouble getting this the first time."

Greg picked up all fifteen copies of the first master, turned them over so the blank side was up, and put them back into the paper tray of the copier. "Now we print the *second* master copy onto the flip side of those fifteen sheets." Pushing the Print button, he said, "First you try a single to make sure it's all good," and he waited until the sheet came out. Maura looked over his shoulder at it.

"Everything seem dark enough?" he asked.

Maura said, "Yeah. Looks good."

"Then watch this."

Greg folded the paper in half lengthwise, then end to end, and then end to end once more, making all the creases sharp and clean. He took the stapler and punched it twice along the center fold of the pages. Maura looked like a kid watching a magician's best trick.

Greg said, "Scissors, please," and Maura handed them to him. He couldn't resist waving the blades around like a magic wand. "Now, the last step."

With a skill and speed that came from having done it hundreds of times before, Greg trimmed off the top, front, and bottom edges.

Then, holding it out to her, he said, "Here . . . the first copy of your first comic book."

Maura took it from him as if it was a rare gem. She sat on the front edge of the desk chair. She stared at the cover, then opened the book and slowly read the first page. Completely absorbed, she looked at every image, drinking in the story, the pictures, everything.

Greg might as well have been ten miles away. And he was fine with that. He pushed the button and the copier began to print the remaining fourteen sheets. And while the machine hummed and

stuttered, Greg leaned against the back of the couch and watched Maura read.

He couldn't remember any other time like this. He knew he had never just sat and looked at somebody else's face before—not for a full minute, then two minutes.

And as he watched Maura's face, seeing what this meant to her, Greg tried to find a word for the feeling he was getting. Because he was definitely getting something.

It was fun, but he knew fun wasn't the right word. It was more than that. Because this experience Maura was having, that he was watching? The fun part was knowing that he'd had a lot to do with it. After she'd snapped at him in the lunchroom on Friday, he could have just walked away—let her flop around with her pictures and her story, let her try to make something on her own. But he hadn't done that. What was happening to Maura at this very moment, it was like a gift—something he'd given to her. On purpose.

Maura finished and looked up into Greg's face. She gave a little laugh and said, "Sorry— guess I zoned out. But it's . . . it's really *something*, don't you think?" Then she smiled.

And at that second, Greg felt like Maura's smile had to be worth at least a million dollars.

Embarrassed by his thoughts, Greg nodded and said, "Yeah . . . really something."

He quickly folded, stapled, and trimmed a second copy of *The Lost Unicorn*. It was his turn to look through it.

It truly was a great little comic. And Greg couldn't help saying, "I've *got* to figure out how to sell this. I could make a *ton* of money!"

Maura narrowed her eyes. "Correction," she said. "You mean, '*We* could make a ton of money.' *We*."

Greg was annoyed by Maura's tone of voice. But honestly, he was only half annoyed. He grinned and nodded. "Sorry. Bad habit. We."

Maura smiled and said, "That's better."

As she continued looking through her comic book, Maura said, "But, really, I don't care that much about the money."

Greg looked at Maura like her brain had just plopped out onto the floor. "You don't *care*? About the *money*? Oh, sure. Like I almost believe that."

"Well, it's true." Maura lifted her chin and said, "But you probably wouldn't understand.

I'm mostly an artist. I just want to make a great comic book."

"And sell it," said Greg. "*And* make money."

Maura sniffed. "The money comes way, way second. Because if my art and my writing isn't good, people won't want the comic, and of course, no one would pay for it. So, to me, the most important thing is that it's good."

Greg nodded. "Right. So it'll make money."

"No," insisted Maura, "so it'll be *good*. Because even if I never made any money, my comic book would still be good. And that's what I really care about."

Greg thought a second and then said, "So you're saying that back when you made all those pot holders, you *weren't* trying to make money?"

Maura tossed her head. "That was different."

Greg smiled. "Ohhh, I see. *Some*times you want to make money, and sometimes you just want to make pot holders because they're so *beau*tiful."

Maura glared at him and said, "If you *have* to know, I made those pot holders because *you* called me brainless, and I wanted to shut you up. And I knew that I could make as much money as you could any day—even more. But even so, those pot holders *were* beautiful. And I *did* make a lot of money. Only it didn't really shut you up. Which is the only bad part."

Greg kept pushing. "Well, what about in the cafeteria the other day, when I said we could make your comic books, *and* sell them. You argued—you did. You argued until I gave you seventy-five percent of the profits. So admit it—you were fighting for more money. For yourself."

"No," Maura said, "I just didn't want you to think you could get away with anything. Because you can't, not with me. And if my comics *do* make money, then *I'm* going to get *my* fair share. But that doesn't mean I'm all crazy about money. Like *some* people."

Greg said, "Well, I don't care what you think. Or what Mr. Z thinks, because he's just like you are. Everybody keeps acting like I shouldn't want to make money. Too bad. I'm *gonna* make money, lots and lots of it. The more the better. And if you and everybody else want to pretend money's not important, that's fine, because that'll mean more for me."

For the next three minutes the two of them

folded, trimmed, and stapled in silence. Then Greg reached over and picked up the small stack of comics Maura had finished. He flipped through them one at a time. "This one's okay. And this one's okay. Uh-oh . . . Look: crooked cutting on this one. And bad stapling on this one. And bad folding. Three out of five rejected. You need another lesson?"

Maura snapped, "Give me those." She looked at the comics Greg had challenged. She said, "What are you talking about? These two are okay. And I could pull out those staples and put some others in straight. Kids would still buy them—I'm sure they would."

Greg shook his head. "Doesn't matter. They're too sloppy. Chunky Comics have to be perfect—or at least a *lot* better than these three are."

Maura nodded contritely, and then she grinned and chortled, "Ha-ha—gotcha!"

"What?" said Greg.

"You *do* care about whether your comics are good. It doesn't matter if kids would buy them anyway, they have to be *good*—that's what you just said."

"Yeah? So what?" said Greg.

"So *you* agree with *me*, that's what. It's not *only* about the money. Is it?" And then Maura smiled and fluttered her eyelids at him.

"That's it," Greg said. "No more talking. Just finish that stack, all right? And be careful. And then *you* can *leave*."

"Aye-aye, sir," Maura said. She held her fingers up in the Girl Scout salute. "And I promise to make every Chunky Comic as *good* as it can possibly be."

"Very funny," Greg said, and he kept his face as hard as iron. Which wasn't easy. And when he turned to pick up the last sheets off the copier, he grinned at the wall. But then he got serious again right away, because one of the printed pages wasn't quite dark enough.

And as he adjusted the copier to reprint another page, he had to admit that Maura was right. It wasn't *only* about the money. Not always. Just most of the time.

Chapter 17

SELLING

Maura took eight copies of her new comic book home from Greg's on Sunday night. She gave one to her mom, one to her dad, and one to her big brother, Tommy. Everyone was impressed.

"Maura!" her mother said. "This is *amazing*! Of course, I always knew you had art talent, but this is a *won*derful little book. Like a fairy tale. And I love unicorns, don't you? I mean, of course you do, because here's the book, and who made it? You did! My Maura is an *author*! This is . . . *amazing*!"

Maura thought so too. And that's why she autographed one copy and tucked it into the zippered pocket of her backpack. And on Monday morning when she went to meet her friend Allyson on the way to the bus stop, she gave it to her. Allyson sat right down on her front steps and read it. And when Allyson was done reading, she said, "This is *so* good!"

Maura beamed and said, "Thanks." As the bus came around the corner, Maura said, "You better leave that at home—just stick it in your mailbox or something."

But Allyson said, "It's okay. I won't show it to anybody. Promise." She slipped it inside the front cover of her social studies book, and then they both ran and got on the bus.

Maura had watched Allyson's face as she'd read the story and looked at the pictures. And sitting on the bus, she started counting kids. There were forty-seven students on the bus by the time they got to school. And Maura found herself thinking a little like Greg. Because she felt sure that she could have sold every single boy and girl on the bus a copy of her new comic book. She could have been well on her way toward being a recognized artist. And author. Except it wasn't allowed.

As usual Mrs. Davenport had been very efficient. She had prepared a written version of the all-school announcement she had made on Friday. She had made it shorter, more to the point, and it was printed up in large type. And by Monday morning a copy was hanging on every bulletin board in every hallway and every classroom at Ashworth Intermediate School.

ANNOUNCEMENT

Some of our students have been making small comic books and then bringing them to school and selling them to their friends. This is not permitted. Our town School Committee has a strict policy about what may and may not be sold at school.

Starting right now, these little comic books may not be <u>brought</u> to school, they may not be <u>created</u> at school, and they certainly may not be <u>sold</u> at school.

Thank you all for your cooperation.
Mrs. Davenport, Principal

Sitting in social studies, Maura stared at a copy of the announcement. She read it, then she read it again. And one sentence stood out to her: *Our town School Committee has a strict policy about what may and may not be sold at school.*

"May and may not." So that meant some things were okay to sell at school, and some things were not. And the School Committee got to choose. Interesting.

In her mind Maura began arguing with the School Committee, imagining what she would say to those people. Because, really, what was wrong with selling their comics to other kids? Nothing—or at least nothing she could see. Certainly not with her little comic book. Or Greg's either.

And sitting there thinking in Mrs. Sanborn's class, Maura happened to look over and notice the front of Brittany's social studies book. Except she couldn't actually see the *World Cultures* book. On the first day of school Mrs. Sanborn had required that all the kids tape covers onto their new books. And the glossy book covers Mrs. Sanborn had handed out were loaded with pictures of high-school athletes wearing Nike shoes and Nike shirts and Nike shorts and hats and warm-ups. And Maura realized that every social studies book in the classroom was trying to sell her something. And she thought, *I guess the School Committee decided that was okay.*

Then in the gym a couple periods later, Maura saw posters about a fund-raiser for new uniforms for the soccer and basketball teams. They weren't posters kids had made. These were large, bright, printed posters, and every one showed beautiful, full-color pictures of M&M's, 3 Musketeers bars, and Skittles. So someone must have decided that it was okay to buy and sell candy at school.

Outside during gym, Maura took a good look at the new scoreboard on the soccer field. It was all red and white, and it was trying to sell her a Coke. Next to the door on the way back inside, a big black-and-blue machine was trying to sell her a bottle of sports drink. And in the cafeteria at lunchtime, a long banner was selling pizza because it was Domino's Pizza Day. And over in the corner, a machine was selling frosty cans of juice.

Seeing all this got Maura thinking. But then during seventh-period language arts class something happened that got Maura really excited. And when she saw Greg in the hall right after school, she ran up, grabbed him by the arm, and blurted out, "Did Mrs. Lindahl pass out something in your language arts class today?"

Greg looked at Maura as if she'd escaped from a zoo. He shook his head, and Maura said, "No? Well, look what Mrs. Pelham passed out last period—to every kid in the room. Here."

Greg took the papers she held out. He looked at the front, flipped it over to look at the back cover, then turned a page, and said, "Yeah . . . so what?"

Maura looked at him, disgusted. "So what? Don't you get it? Think about what Mrs. Davenport said. About selling stuff at school. About selling comic books. Now look again."

Greg looked again, and this time he got it.

Because what Greg held in his hands was the new flyer from the book club—a full-color, eight-page advertisement. The ad was selling books, more than seventy-five different titles. There were classics and there were Newbery award winners. But there were also Garfield and X-Men books, and Scooby-Doo cartoon books, and Calvin and Hobbes collections. There were magic-trick books, drawing books, and even books that came with toys—like bobble-head key chains and little silver necklaces.

This book-club flyer was like all the other ones Greg had looked at once a month, ever since first grade. Because once a month, the teachers handed out the flyers, and then the kids placed their orders. And then the teachers collected the money.

And where did all this buying and selling happen? At school.

Chapter 18

COMPLICATED

Three minutes after Maura showed Greg the book-club flyer, they rushed into Mr. Z's room, and Maura said, "Mr. Z! We've *got* to ask you something."

Startled, Mr. Z looked up from the quizzes he was grading. "Oh—sure. About math?" he said hopefully.

Greg shook his head. "Look." He put the flyer on the teacher's desk, and pointed at the book of Garfield comics. "How come it's okay for kids to buy books like *that* here at school, but it's *not* okay for us to sell our mini–comic books?"

Mr. Z picked up the flyer and flipped through it. "Hmmm." He had seen packets of these in the office by the teacher mailboxes, but they always went to the reading and language arts teachers, never to him. "Very interesting."

"So?" said Maura. "Does the book club have

special permission from the School Committee or something?"

Mr. Z nodded. "I guess they must."

Maura said, "Well, then it's not fair. Because our comics aren't so different from some of these books. And they're selling them right here at school. Here. Take a look at this." Maura had borrowed back her new copy of *The Lost Unicorn* from Allyson, and she handed it to Mr. Z. "Greg and I finished it this weekend. And I know it's not supposed to be here at school. But it's been hidden away all day. And I just wanted you to see it. Because it's good, and it's not even violent."

Mr. Z began to thumb through the comic. The drawings were exceptional, especially for student work. Remembering Mrs. Davenport, he glanced toward his doorway, and then quickly flipped through the rest of the pages. Maura was right. There was less violence in this comic book than there was in a lot of classic fairy tales. And looking at the credits on the back cover, he saw that these two former enemies had apparently worked together.

Mr. Z smiled and nodded his approval, and immediately Maura said, "So we want special permission too. Like the book clubs. To sell our comics. Who should we talk to?"

Mr. Z looked from Maura's face to Greg's. He could see there was no point in trying to talk them out of this. He took a deep breath and decided to try anyway. "Well, the School Committee has a meeting once a month. But the principals of each school are always at the meetings. And you already know how Mrs. Davenport feels about comic books." Then handing the little book back to Maura, he said, "And please, put that away."

"But what about *these* comics?" said Greg, pointing at the flyer again. "She's letting these be bought and sold at school. So that's not fair."

Mr. Z nodded. "I'm not saying you're wrong. I'm just telling you that what you're asking is . . . well, it's complicated."

Mr. Z pulled a handful of papers from the in-box on his desk, flipped through five or six sheets, and then said, "The School Committee meets this Thursday night at seven thirty in the municipal building. And I guess if you wanted to go and talk to them, there's nothing stopping you. But . . . it's complicated."

Greg shook his head. "You keep saying 'complicated, complicated.' Why? We're just asking for the same deal the book club is getting. What's so complicated about that?"

"Well," said Mr. Z, "for one thing, book clubs are big companies, and I know they have teachers and librarians and reading experts working for them, helping to pick the books. And on the back of the flyer here it says that teachers get free books for their classrooms when they send in the orders. So the book clubs help teachers. Plus, they're helping kids learn, and getting them excited about reading and books. And you're just a couple of kids who want to sell some little comics and maybe make some money."

Greg said, "But aren't the book clubs making money?"

Mr. Z nodded. "I'm sure they are."

"So there's still no difference," said Greg. "And we can give away free copies of our comics to teachers too. That's not a problem."

"Yeah," said Maura. "And . . . and we'll even give some of our profits to the school library fund—ten percent of our profits for buying new library books."

"What?" said Greg. This girl was giving money away—*his* money.

Maura ignored him. "So what do you think, Mr. Z? Don't you think we have a chance?"

"Well . . . I suppose so," he said.

"Great!" said Maura, "'Cause I already told Greg how on Friday you said you could help us. With business stuff. So this is great. What should we do first?"

Mr. Z gulped. "Oh . . . you mean . . . um . . . Well, I really don't think I could . . . I mean . . ." Mr. Z looked from Maura's face to Greg's, and then back to Maura's. And he saw there was no way out.

So he decided to stall for time. "Well, I guess . . . first, I'd better do a little thinking—all of us should. And you should both talk to your parents about this, because they ought to know what you're thinking about doing. So how about we all take some time, and then we can get together again. To compare our notes. How's that sound?"

Maura made a face. "It sounds slow. Because the School Committee meeting is Thursday night. So we have to meet again tomorrow. Before school. Like at seven thirty."

Greg nodded. "Before school. Okay, Mr. Z? See ya tomorrow."

And both kids turned and rushed out, Greg to soccer practice, and Maura to catch her bus.

Sitting there at his desk, Mr. Z felt like he'd been run over by a couple of go-carts. He tried to remember what he'd been doing only two minutes earlier. *Oh, yes—grading quizzes.* He picked up his red pen.

But Mr. Z couldn't concentrate. And even the peace and quiet of room 27 didn't help. Sure, it was calm and orderly now. But he had an uneasy feeling—the kind that comes just before a storm.

Chapter 19

PLANNING

On Tuesday morning Mr. Z sat in his room, secretly hoping that Greg and Maura wouldn't show up, hoping something might have derailed their plan. Like maybe a big *No!* from somebody's mom or dad. Or maybe a sudden outbreak of common sense. Or even a flat tire on a school bus—something, anything.

But at exactly 7:30 Maura walked into the math room and said, "Hi, Mr. Z." She sat at a desk and began digging around in her backpack. She pulled out a pencil and then a new spiral notebook. She opened it to the first page and carefully wrote the date and the time. She looked up at Mr. Z and said, "I'm going to keep a record. Of our meetings."

About a minute later Greg walked in. Maura looked at him and said, "You're late. It's not businesslike to be late." She turned and wrote something in her notebook.

Greg made a face at the back of her head. Turning to Mr. Z, he said, "So what should we do first?"

Mr. Z said, "First, I need to know what your parents think about all this."

Greg said, "Mine are fine with it, with talking to the School Committee and everything. They're gonna come to the meeting, at least my dad is for sure, and my mom's gonna try to cancel another meeting she has for Thursday. But they both think it's fine, especially after I showed them the flyer from the book club."

Maura nodded. "My parents think it's okay too. Only my mom more than my dad. He thinks it's sort of crazy. But they both said to thank you for helping. And they're both coming to the meeting too."

Mr. Z took a deep breath and let it out slowly. Now there was truly no way out. He felt trapped. He honestly wanted to help these kids. And he honestly saw nothing wrong with either their comic books or their wish to make them available to their friends. It even seemed okay to make a little money. But sometime soon he knew he would have to talk to the principal.

Mr. Z had spent most of his life carefully avoiding disagreements and disputes. First in grade school, and then right through high school, college, and graduate school, he had learned to keep away from controversy. Because any situation that might include yelling could easily lead to pushing, and pushing sometimes led to all sorts of unpleasantness. Even *b-l-o-o-d*.

But this current situation had conflict written all over it. He certainly didn't imagine that Mrs. Davenport was going to haul off and sock him in the nose or anything, but as he thought of facing her and explaining his involvement in this business, his hands began to sweat.

Then Mr. Z had a good thought—another way out. He said, "Well, one thing I have to do as soon as possible is call the superintendent's office and ask if they have any room on the agenda for Thursday's meeting. We might need to wait a month. Maybe we're too late."

"But maybe we're not," Maura said, "so I think we should go ahead and get ready anyway."

Greg nodded. "Yeah, like we need a whole plan of what we say, and who says what. Because we really have to look like we know what we're doing, or I bet they won't even listen to us."

"Then I think I should talk first," Maura said. "Because I know exactly what we want to ask permission for."

Greg snorted. "You? Why you? I know what we want. This whole thing was my idea, remember? I should talk first."

"*Your* idea?" said Maura. "*I* was the one who saw the book-club flyer—and when I showed it to you, you didn't even see the point until after I told you. So don't start acting like this is all about you."

"Oh, *right*," Greg said, "because everybody knows that you're such a great—"

WHAM! Mr. Z slapped his right hand flat onto his desk. "*Enough*! I thought you two had gotten past this. And if you haven't, then just get up and leave, both of you."

After a few seconds of silence Greg said,

"Sorry. I mean, if everyone wants Maura to talk first, that's fine with me."

And Maura said, "No, it's okay. I don't have to talk first. That was stupid."

Greg thought, *Yeah, really stupid,* but he kept his eyes on Mr. Z's face. Because he knew that without the math teacher's help, this idea was going nowhere.

Glad to see the immediate change in attitude, and pleased with himself for being so forceful, Mr. Z became the self-appointed chairperson of their little meeting. For the next twenty-five minutes they had a lively, friendly exchange of ideas—as Maura took furious notes.

And Mr. Z actually enjoyed himself. True, there was a dull ache in his right hand from whacking his desk, but the plan that started taking shape didn't seem crazy or dangerous or hopeless. In it's own weird way, it made perfect sense.

As the bell rang for homeroom, Maura believed that she might actually get the chance to have all the other kids at school read her stories and see her artwork. Mr. Z believed that the clear, almost mathematical logic of the proposal might actually convince the School Committee that this was a good idea. And Greg believed that maybe, just maybe, Chunky Comics might actually make him a whole bunch of money.

Chapter 20

AGENDAS

It was about twelve thirty on Wednesday afternoon, right in the middle of Mr. Z's preparation period. He was writing short equations on the board, one for every student in his next class.

Mrs. Davenport appeared in the doorway of room 27 and said, "If you have a minute, I'd like you to explain something for me."

Mr. Z knew that voice. He turned around and saw the principal waving a sheet of blue paper.

"Sure . . . what's that?" he asked.

She took a few steps into the room. "It's the agenda for tomorrow night's School Committee meeting. And there's an item under New Business: 'Students and faculty advisor to propose new comic-book club at Ashworth Intermediate School.'"

"Oh," said Mr. Z. "That. I hadn't heard

anything yet. I was hoping that the School Committee wouldn't even consider the request. But it looks like they did." The math teacher felt his hands begin to sweat.

Mrs. Davenport said, "Let me guess: The students are Greg Kenton and Maura Shaw, and the faculty advisor is you. Right?"

Mr. Z nodded. "And I had planned to talk to you just as soon as I found out if the committee was going to accept a presentation. Because I didn't want to cause . . . a stir. Not if it wasn't necessary."

Mrs. Davenport smiled at his choice of words. She waved the blue sheet again and said, "And now it's necessary. So talk to me."

"Well," said Mr. Z, "you know these two kids—both of them so smart. And they figured

out that it's the School Committee who sets the policy about selling things in the schools— it was right there in your announcement. And they think their little comics are as good as some of the books the kids can buy here at school from the book clubs every month. So they want to make their case. And I sort of told them I'd help. That's all."

Mrs. Davenport was still smiling faintly. "You offered to help? Even though you knew my opinion about all this?"

Mr. Z said, "I didn't exactly volunteer. But when they told me what they wanted to do, I guess I decided to stay involved. To try to represent the best interests of the school."

Mrs. Davenport's eyebrows went up. "'Represent the best interests of the school'? You didn't think I was already doing that?"

Mr. Z said, "Well, not exactly."

The principal's eyebrows went up a notch higher. Mr. Z had been dreading this moment, but he knew what he had to say. He gulped and went on. "I don't think there's anything wrong with comic books—with the good ones, that is. And the ones these kids are making aren't bad. And they're definitely creative.

And maybe other kids should get a chance to read them."

Mrs. Davenport nodded. "Ah . . . I didn't know that you'd become a reading expert."

There was a long, awkward pause. Mr. Z practically held his breath, afraid to guess what was coming. When it came, he was completely surprised.

Because Mrs. Davenport slowly shook her head from side to side, and then began to chuckle. "A reading expert." Then she smiled broadly.

Mr. Z began to breathe again.

She said, "Well, Mr. Zenotopoulous, I thank you for your pioneering work as a reading specialist, and also for keeping watch over our young tycoons. And I'll be there tomorrow night to hear the presentation. And who knows? I just might have an agenda of my own—to represent the best interests of the school."

And with that she turned and left, chuckling all the way back to her office.

Chapter 21

THE QUESTION OF MONEY

Thursday afternoon was scraping along like a glacier. Greg looked at the clock again. Not even four minutes had passed. It was still almost the beginning of fifth period. Mrs. Chalmers was teaching them a new piece of music, and she was working with the sopranos first. Then came the altos. And then finally, the tenors would get a turn. At this rate the school day was going to drag on for another month, maybe two.

Tonight was the night of the School Committee meeting, and Greg couldn't wait. He was eager to stand up and talk to the grown-ups, a whole crowd of them. He was going to state his case. He might even have an argument. That part was exciting to him. Greg was dying to see what everyone would think about the comic-book club.

But more than that, Greg wanted the whole

thing to be over, finished, settled one way or the other. He wanted it to be over so he could think about something else. Because for a solid week now, he'd been thinking about nothing but money. And during that week, money had become much more complicated.

Until his big blowup with Maura, and then his run-ins with Mr. Z and Mrs. Davenport, the question of money had been simple for Greg. In fact, it hadn't even been a question. Money was money, and money was great. It was good to make it, good to have it, good to save it, and it was always good to want more and more and more of it. Money? Simple.

Also, Greg's attitude about money used to be private. Until he had started trying to sell Chunky Comics, how he made his money and what he chose to do with it was nobody's business but his.

And tonight he was going to have to stand up in public and try to tell all these people why he ought to be allowed to sell his comics and make some money at school.

It helped that Maura was in on the deal, and Mr. Z, too. But Greg knew they didn't think about money the way he did. They thought *he* was a nutcase, a money maniac—a moneyac. And tonight what if everybody else thought so too? And worse than that, what if it was actually true?

Greg thought, *Maybe I really <u>am</u> a greedy little money-grubber. Maybe I really <u>don't</u> care about anybody but myself. "Ladies and gentlemen, meet Greg Kenton, the greediest, most selfish kid on earth."*

Greg looked at Mrs. Chalmers. She was going over and over the same sixteen notes with the sopranos, smiling, nodding, playing the piano, and singing along. It looked like hard work. *And I know she doesn't make a lot of money,* he thought. *None of my teachers do.*

And that reminded Greg of his conversation with Mr. Z about other jobs. Greg knew Mr. Z could be making tons more money if he worked for a lab or an engineering company. But instead he was a math teacher. And that thing he'd said about his brother, the low-paid doctor: for him, enough is enough.

And ever since that conversation, Greg had thought about Mr. Z's toilet theory at least four times a day.

And three days ago Greg had heard on the

evening news that Bill Gates, one of the richest men in the world, was giving away another 375 million dollars for education in Africa. Superrich, and giving his money away. And in that same news story, they told how Ted Turner, the man who started CNN, had given one billion dollars to the United Nations—a *billion*.

Money thoughts had been following him everywhere—around the school, onto the soccer field, across town to his home, even into the bathroom. Greg couldn't get away from them. But if this slow-motion school day would ever end, and if tonight's School Committee meeting would ever arrive, maybe that could change.

Chapter 22

NEW BUSINESS

At 9:20 on Thursday night Greg sat next to his dad and mom near the back of the meeting room in the municipal building. He sat up extra straight once in a while, trying to see the small group of principals, because Mr. Z had said they would be here. And in the second or third row, down near the front, he was pretty sure he'd spotted the back of Mrs. Davenport's head.

Greg squirmed on the folding chair, twisting his neck from side to side. He couldn't get comfortable. He had on a blue sport coat, a pair of itchy gray pants, a white shirt, his best black shoes, and a red necktie borrowed from his brother Ross.

Dressing up was Maura's idea. Greg had complained, but she had insisted. "What—do you want to look like some kid who just came in from the playground?"

Maura sat three chairs away. She was wearing a dark blue pants suit and a white shirt with a small ruffle at the neck—her new business outfit, bought especially for the occasion. Then came Mr. and Mrs. Shaw, and at the other end of the row, Mr. Z sat next to Greg.

Greg decided that his math teacher was just as twitchy as he was. They had all been sitting, waiting, fidgeting for almost two hours.

Greg had seen School Committee meetings on the local cable TV channel, but he had always flipped right past. And now he knew why. These people talked and talked and talked—health care for teachers, new science books, snow plowing, special-education grants, state funding for tests, roof repairs—on and on and on.

Greg whispered to Mr. Z, "How much does the town pay the School Committee?"

Mr. Z held up his right hand with the tips of his thumb and forefinger pressed together.

At first Greg didn't get it. Then he whispered, "Zero?"

Mr. Z nodded.

So there it was again: All the people in the world were caring, noble volunteers. Except for Greg Kenton, who was selfish and greedy.

The note cards Greg held had been rolled, unrolled, bent, chewed on, and twisted until the black ink had turned gray and smudgy. But it didn't matter, because Greg had planned out exactly what he was going to say anyway. And he got to talk first because he had won the coin toss—heads—a victory over Maura. But at the moment he was wishing he had called tails.

As Greg began going over his opening statement for the ninth time, the chairperson of the School Committee said, "For the next item under New Business, we have a proposal about . . . a comic-book club at Ashworth School. Who's speaking on this?"

Greg bounced to his feet and managed to say, "I . . . I am."

The chairperson pointed. "Please come up to the table and talk into the microphone."

Maura thought Greg looked very nice tonight in his blazer and his gray slacks. His black eye was almost gone, and she was pretty sure he had even tried to brush his hair.

As Greg went down the center aisle, he got a good look at Mrs. Davenport sitting in the second row with the other principals. She wasn't smiling.

Greg handed a copy of *Return of the Hunter* and a copy of *The Lost Unicorn* to each of the five committee members. He also gave each of them a book-club flyer.

Greg sat at the table in front of the microphone. A woman from the local cable channel turned on a video camera, and a small red light began blinking at him. Greg tried to smile into the camera, but his mouth was so dry his lips got stuck on his front teeth. His pounding heart made it feel like he had a squirrel running around under his shirt.

The microphone was high, so Greg pulled one leg up under him, cleared his throat, leaned forward, and rattled off his first sentence in a loud, squeaky voice. "I'm Greg Kenton, and I go to Ashworth Intermediate School." Greg gulped, and forced himself to talk slower and lower. "I started making little comic books over the summer." He held up the Creon comic. "This was the first one. And in September I took some copies to school and I sold them to my friends, one for a quarter. And every-body liked them. But I didn't know I had to have permis-sion from the School Committee to sell  things at school. Until Mrs. Davenport told me. So that's what I'm here to ask for."

Holding up a copy of *The Lost Unicorn*, Greg said, "Maura Shaw, she lives across the street from me, and she made this comic—I helped her. And now we both want to make more. I call them Chunky Comics. And we think kids will like them . . . because they're fun to read. Kids could even collect them."

Greg held up the book-club flyer, and noticed that his hand was shaking. "Every month at our school some of the teachers give kids an ad like this, mostly in language arts or reading class. There are all kinds of books in here, and on the back there's an order form. And kids choose what they want, and then they bring money to school, and they buy the books. And kids really like it. So we want to do the same thing—sell our comic books to kids at school."

That was the cue for Maura to stand up. Greg turned stiffly and pointed at her. "Maura Shaw will now explain the way our comic-book club would work." Greg got up and headed toward a chair on the left side of the room as Maura walked to the front.

If Maura was nervous, she didn't show it. From a file folder cradled in one arm, she took a slim stack of stapled pages and handed one packet to each committee member. She walked to the table, sat lightly on the front edge of the chair, spread some papers out in front of her, and said, "Good evening" into the microphone. She nodded and smiled at the camera and then to each of the committee members.

Holding up her copy of the packet, she said, "Please look at the first page of the information

I handed you. This is a sample order form for the Chunky Comics Club. Right now, there are only two titles available, the ones that Greg handed to you. There would be a

new order form every month, unless there weren't any new titles. Just like a regular book club, teachers get to choose whether or not they want to be part of our club. And just like a book club, when kids order comics, teachers get to order copies for free, to have in their classrooms."

Maura looked up at the committee members. She said, "Please turn to page two."

Greg was impressed with Maura's performance so far. No goof-ups. No shakiness. No drooling. Just about perfect. Except she looked like she was twenty-three years old. And was that *makeup* on her face? Or was it just the way her cheeks looked when she got excited about something? Because he'd noticed that before.

Papers rustled, and Maura said, "Our comic-book club also wants to do something different. If we make any money selling our comics at school, we want to donate part of that money to the new-book fund of our school library—ten percent of all the profits."

Maura moved on to page three. "We know there are other kids at our school who are good at writing and drawing. So we want to have some after-school workshops, and maybe help other kids to be creative too. And that might mean there would be more comics, and maybe other kinds of books or stories for the Chunky Comics Club."

Maura slowly turned the page, lifted up the packet, and made a dramatic pause. Gently waving the sheet back and forth, she said, "This last page is important. Regular book clubs are careful about picking the right kind of books to sell to different aged kids. We're going to be careful too. Everybody knows that some of the comic books at stores are really violent. Chunky Comics won't be like that. Everything sold by our club is going be approved in advance by teachers. Mr. Zenotopoulous said he would be one of those teachers, and Mrs. Lindahl said she would help too. And now our advisor, Mr. Zenotopoulous, would like to say a few words."

Mr. Z made his way to the front of the room, and Maura moved over to sit by Greg.

Mr. Z had no handouts. He sat down in front of the microphone and said, "I know it must seem like Greg and Maura are making a strange request. At first, I thought so too.

"As all of you know, I teach math. And I tend to think that way—mathematically. And the more I've looked at what Greg and Maura are asking, everything adds up. It's completely logical. The book clubs have permission to sell books directly to kids at school. These clubs sell all kinds of books, including ones about cartoon and comic-book characters. So Greg and Maura want permission to do the same.

"They have been creative and responsible, and they've found an interesting way to use the skills they have developed at school—in reading, writing, art, history, science, and of course, math. As teachers, we try to prepare kids for life after they leave school, for the time when they go out and earn money and become contributing members of the economy and the society. So I think it's great that these kids are doing this right now, at their own level, in a positive and practical way. And I don't see any conflict at all with the skills and the values our schools are trying to teach."

Mr. Z took a deep breath, and then said, "I know some people don't think comic books are good for children. With your permission, I'd like to use a little math right here. I've been sitting in the back of the room, and I have counted forty-one grown-ups at this meeting. So I am asking for a show of hands, please: How many of us used to read comic books once in a while when we were in elementary or middle school?"

Greg looked over the audience and quickly counted twenty-nine hands. Among the small cluster of principals, only two did not raise their hands. And Mrs. Davenport was one of them.

Mr. Z made a note on a small pad of paper. Then he said, "Hands down, please. That was seventy-one percent of the grown-ups in the room. Now, how many of us read cartoon books when we were children or young teens—cartoons like Peanuts, or Garfield, or maybe Disney characters?" All but six hands went up.

Mr. Z made a note, a quick scribble, and said, "That's eighty-five percent of us."

Then Mr. Z said, "And how many of us regularly looked at comics or cartoons in newspapers or magazines when we were between the ages of eight and twelve?" One hundred percent of the hands in the room went up, even Mrs. Davenport's.

Mr. Z turned and smiled at the committee. "There's my proof. Apparently comic books and cartoons do not have the power to keep children from growing up to become responsible citizens like us—the kind of people who run schools and school districts, and decide how to spend millions of tax dollars every year. And I believe that the kids at our school will not be harmed by this Chunky Comics Club. If anything, I think they'll be inspired and engaged in a lot of constructive ways. So I rest my case, and as Maura said, I'm happy to be one of the teachers who makes sure that every item presented by this club is appropriate."

Mr. Z nodded at the committee members, said, "Thank you," then stood up and walked back to his seat.

The chairperson put a hand over her microphone and leaned first left and then right to whisper to the other members of the committee. Then she said, "Thank you, Mr. Zenotopoulous, and thank you, Greg and Maura, for your interesting presentation. The committee would like to take some time to consider this request before voting. It's getting late, so if there is no other discussion, we can move on to the last item under New Business, the contract with the food-service company for the high school."

Greg watched the chairperson as she looked out across the room. And Greg saw her eyes stop, saw her face change, saw that she was about to call on someone. Because someone wanted more discussion about the Chunky Comics Club.

Without even looking, Greg knew who it was. And he was right.

It was Mrs. Davenport.

Chapter 23

THE BEST INTERESTS OF THE SCHOOL

Mrs. Davenport stood up and walked to the front table. Greg couldn't believe how small she looked. Seeing her walking around in a room full of other grown-ups, she only looked about half as big as she did at school.

But when she began to talk, Mrs. Davenport seemed larger than life, just like always. She nodded toward Greg and Maura and said, "It was good to hear students from my school speak so clearly and intelligently. And it was good to hear my colleague Mr. Zenotopoulous speak as well. He and I have worked together for over twelve years now, and I have great respect for his talent and his love of the teaching profession. But I feel I must add something to what he's said.

"I did not read comic

books when I was a child, and neither did any of my brothers or sisters. Comic books were forbidden at our home. We had plenty of things to read, but always books—real picture books and chapter books and novels. My mother felt that comic books were 'cheap and trashy'—those are her exact words. On long car trips she read aloud to us—books like *Tom Sawyer* and *Charlotte's Web* and *The Swiss Family Robinson*—lots and lots of great books.

"We were not allowed to watch Saturday morning cartoons at my home either. Back then, I thought all of this was unfair. But by the time I reached college, I felt certain that a childhood without comic books and TV cartoons had been better and richer, not poorer. And as an elementary- and intermediate-school principal for the past eighteen years, I have tried to uphold the highest standards of literacy in our libraries and classrooms.

"But before I go on, I have to make a confession. When I arrived home from school late yesterday afternoon, there was a package waiting for me. I don't know who sent it, because there was no mailing label, no return address. When I opened the box, first I discovered this note: 'Please take a good look.' And under the note this is what I found."

Mrs. Davenport walked back to her chair, leaned over, reached into a box, and then held up a small stack of comic books.

Standing in the aisle and facing the audience, she said, "There were twenty or thirty of these in the box. My husband was thrilled, because he remembered some of these from when he was a boy. And with some encouragement from him, I sat at home last night and I read comic books for the first time in my life. And here is my confession: I enjoyed myself.

"Please don't misunderstand me. Nothing will ever convince me that *Three Supermen from Krypton* or *Donald Duck in Volcano Valley* can be called great children's literature. But I am ready to agree that a good comic book can be fun—and basically harmless, as Mr. Zenotopoulous said."

Greg was almost floating up out of his chair. He nudged Maura and whispered, "This is great!"

But the principal wasn't done.

Mrs. Davenport went back to the microphone and paused to look into the faces of the committee members. "However, I believe we have to think carefully about this question of what gets sold to children at our schools. And especially what children sell to one another. What if a student decides next week that she wants to set up a stand to sell her homemade dolls out by the buses before and after school? Will you give her permission? Or what if a boy decides to bring his baseball-card collection to school so he can wheel and deal between classes? Try to imagine all the different things that children could dream up to sell to each other. Do we want our school to turn into a huge flea market? How can we give permission to this plan, and then not accept others? As a principal, it is up to me to make sure that my school continues to be a place for learning, not a place for buying and selling."

Greg looked around. A lot of people agreed with what Mrs. Davenport had just said.

Mr. Z raised his hand. The chairperson nodded at him, and he stood up and said, "I agree with everything Mrs. Davenport is saying. School shouldn't become a place that's *all* about buying and selling. But it's *partly* about buying and selling, and we can't pretend it's not. Schools are supposed to prepare kids for a happy, successful life. And one important goal of our school system is to turn out graduates who have something of value they can offer to the world—skills and talents and abilities that others will eventually pay them for. A math teacher gets paid money for teaching math, a principal gets paid money for running a school, and we all hope our students will one day be paid for their work too. So there's certainly nothing wrong with having kids learn about money and economics and profits and percentages. In fact, it would be wrong if we *didn't* teach them these things. Which is why we teach units on the economy and consumer education.

"What Greg and Maura have to offer should help other kids enjoy reading, just like the book clubs do. And their comics even go a step further, because these minicomics will encourage student writing and student artwork. The regular book club companies provide a wholesome service that supports education, and that's why they're allowed to sell books at school and make a profit. And everyone agrees that it's right to get paid for work that's done well.

These kids are asking for the same privilege, plus they've volunteered to donate a percentage of all their profits to the school library—which no book club has offered to do."

Mrs. Davenport shook her head. "I still have trouble with the idea of actually selling things right at school."

"But that's already happening," Mr. Z said. He turned to Greg and Maura. "How many different companies did we find that are advertising or selling things directly to kids at Ashworth School?"

Greg said, "A lot."

Maura nodded and started counting them off on her fingers. "There's the Domino's Pizza Day banner in the cafeteria, the Veryfine juice machine, the Frito-Lay snack machine, the POWERade machine by the gym door, the Coca-Cola scoreboard on the playing field, the Nike book covers on all our social studies books, the Mars candy fund-raiser posters in the gym, the Wilson and Spalding and Adidas names on all the sports equipment, and the big IBM letters on every clock in every room in the school."

Greg said, "And there are tons of ads in all

the magazines for kids in the school library, plus all the sports biography books that are like ads for pro sports teams or NASCAR. And sometimes there are morning PA announcements about after-school bake sales or Saturday car washes at the high school. And there's the blue sweatshirt with the Champion logo that Mr. Kellet wears during every gym class. And the Apple logo on almost every computer. And then there's the stuff sold at the school store. Plus the book clubs."

Mr. Z turned to the committee members and said, "I don't like the way children are treated as sales targets, and I know none of you do either. But we have to face it: Selling to children is big business, and we have to help kids understand this so they can make good decisions. I did some research, and do you know how much of their own money American kids in grades kindergarten through six spend every year? Thirteen *billion* dollars—that's billion, with a *b*—thirteen *billion* dollars of their own money. And that number grows every year."

Greg was stunned. *Thirteen billion dollars!*

A week ago Greg would have enjoyed that number. He'd have let that number slowly absorb his entire mind. He would have let himself dream of grabbing huge hunks of that thirteen billion dollars for himself. But tonight the number struck him differently.

Greg suddenly saw that his giant plan for Chunky Comics was no more than a tiny speck, an almost invisible atom on the edge of a huge, whirling universe of money and products, of buying and selling.

Kids spent thirteen _billion_ dollars last year. And part of that was spent by _me_. Greg kept careful records. He knew that during the past twelve months he had spent over four hundred dollars of his own money—the biggest chunk for a new iPod. *Because I'm a sales target, me and every other kid in America—Mr. Z just said so.*

And sitting there at the front of the meeting room, Greg realized that he'd been thinking of the kids at school that same way, as targets. He was the hunter, and they were the prey. And what did he want from the School Committee tonight? A hunting license. He wanted permission to aim his comic books at every kid in the school.

And why? Was it to help kids become better readers? Or to help them get interested in writing and drawing? Not really. Greedy Greg wanted to sell Chunky Comics so he could make money.

Mr. Z was still talking.

"I'm glad that Greg and Maura got to sit through this whole meeting tonight. I'm proud to have them see how much care goes into every detail of what happens in our schools. And I want them to see that this is not 'us against Mrs. Davenport,' because that's not the way it works. We *all* want the same thing—what's best for the school, and what's best for every student."

Greg looked over at Mrs. Davenport, and she was nodding. And Greg felt himself nodding too.

Mr. Z said, "This idea that Greg and Maura have, it's not some marketing plan that was drawn up in Los Angeles or Minneapolis or New York. It's homegrown. So I say it deserves our support. And whatever the School Committee decides will be all right with me and with Greg and with Maura—but only if it's all right with Mrs. Davenport, too. Because we're all in this together."

Mr. Z sat down, and Mrs. Davenport said, "I want to thank Mr. Zenotopoulous for that offer to work together on this, and I accept it. And we'll wait to hear the decision of the committee."

As Mrs. Davenport stood and walked toward her seat, Maura got up and headed for the back of the room. Greg started to follow, but then he stopped. He turned and faced the committee again.

"Could I say something else?" he asked.

The chairperson nodded at him, and Greg went to the microphone. He didn't know exactly what he wanted to say. But he was sure of one thing, so that's what he said first. He gulped and said, "If it's okay, I think I want to sort of change my idea." Greg felt the whole room get very quiet.

The woman squinted and looked over the top of her glasses at him. "You mean the comic-book club? Change it? Now?"

Greg gulped again and said, "Yeah . . . I mean, yes. Because what Mrs. Davenport said is right. It's not fair if Maura and I get special permission to sell our comic books, but then other kids can't sell things they try to make."

A man at the front table said, "So what are you proposing?"

Greg said, "Well . . . I think . . . really . . . there ought to be a way . . . like, if we . . ."

Greg heard himself sputtering and stalling, saying nothing. And he knew why. He didn't really *have* a new idea. But he felt like something needed to change. And he knew it was now or never.

From behind him a voice said, "I think Greg's trying to say that the school store could be the answer." Greg turned around, and it was Mr. Z.

Greg nodded slowly, and then whipped back to face the School Committee. Excited now, he said, "Yeah. That's right. Exactly. It's the school store." And making it up as he went along, Greg said, "Because we already have it. A store. At school. In the cafeteria. Except . . . instead of just school supplies, we can sell our comics there. And . . . and other kids could sell things there too. Because lots of kids have good ideas. And the store can be like a business. A real business. Except . . . any kids who sell stuff at the store have to give . . . fifty percent. Fifty percent of all their profits has to go to something that helps the whole school. Because that way, it'll be half for profit, and half for learning. And . . . and that's my new idea. If it's okay."

Then Greg stood up, turned around, and headed for his seat. As he walked past the principal, he glanced at her face. She was smiling, and he smiled back. And she said, "Just a moment, Greg." She bent over, picked up a small cardboard box, and held it out to him—the old comic books. "I won't be needing these anymore."

Greg blushed, and started to say something back, but the chairperson was calling for the next speaker. Greg gave the principal an awkward smile, took the box, and hurried back to his chair.

As Mrs. Davenport sat down she couldn't help thinking, *He's really a remarkable boy—I'm proud of him.*

And as Greg sat down with the box of comics on his lap, he couldn't help thinking, *Thirteen billion dollars!*

Chapter 24

SUCCESS

The School Committee meeting lasted another fifteen minutes. When it was over, the Kentons and the Shaws and Mr. Z walked out into the parking lot together, and Mrs. Shaw said, "How about we all go over to the Route Twenty-five Diner and celebrate with some ice cream—our treat."

Mr. Z stopped beside his car and took out his keys. "Thanks, but I have to get home."

"But the rest of us can still go, right?" said Greg.

His dad said, "Well, if Mr. Zenotopoulous can't come, then I think we'd better not." He reached out to shake Mr. Z's hand. "You did a great job in there."

Mr. Z smiled and shook his head, pushing the praise aside. Nodding at Greg and Maura, he said, "The congratulations belong to these two. And I really like what Greg said about the school store idea. I think the committee did too, but there's still Mrs. Davenport."

Maura said, "But you heard her—she likes comics now." Pointing at the box in Greg's hands, she said, "And taking those to her house? *That* was genius!"

Greg smiled and said, "Yeah, but—"

Maura cut him off. "No, really, that was a *great* idea, because if she hadn't read them, and if she'd just stood up and screamed and shouted about how awful comic books are—"

Greg shook his head and said, "Sure, but—"

"I'm serious," Maura said. "That was *the* best idea—except for when you said you'd give half our profits to the school. So I say we should still go and get ice cream, and Greg gets to pick anything he wants, even a double banana split, because he—"

Almost shouting, Greg said, "Would you just *be quiet* a second?"

Mr. Z popped open the back of his car. "Greg's trying to tell you that those comics aren't his." He took the box from Greg and put it in his trunk. "I drove over to my mom's home after school yesterday, and I hunted around up in the attic until I found my old comics—two big boxes. Then on my way home I decided to make a special delivery. And I was pretty sure Mrs. Davenport would like my taste in comic books—because there's no *b-l-o-o-d*." He slammed the trunk lid and then smiled at the group. "But no telling, okay? Mrs. Davenport thinks I'm crazy enough already."

Three days later when the School Committee vote was announced, no one was surprised that permission had been granted to Greg Kenton and Maura Shaw to begin selling Chunky Comics at a newly reorganized Ashworth school store—provided that Mrs. Davenport agreed to all the details.

And after some spirited negotiations in the principal's office, no one was surprised that a workable business plan for the store was developed, and a trial period of two months was agreed to. Mrs. Davenport even agreed to be a member of the product approval committee.

Mr. Z helped set up an accounting system for the school store, and Greg and Maura opened a joint savings account at the bank under the name Chunky Comics Group.

Greg and Maura made good on their promise to hold after-school workshops about how to make minicomics and mini–picture books. And soon they had to take on the additional challenge of being editors—choosing which stories and art to accept, and which to reject. Plus they spent time after school helping to get the new school store set up in a semipermanent location in one corner of the cafeteria.

It wasn't always fun, and there was a lot of hard work, but soon the milestones began to drop into place:

- By mid-October the restructured school store had a grand opening. To start, there was a literature section, an arts-and-crafts section, a used-CD section, a collectibles section, plus the regular school supplies. Chunky Comics were sold from a rack built by Greg and painted by Maura.

- Twelve new product ideas for the school store were presented to the product approval committee during the first month of operation. Five were accepted.

- By mid-November, the three elementary schools in town, the junior high, and the high school had all restructured their school stores or started new ones based on the business model pioneered at Ashworth Intermediate School. The Chunky Comics rack was a popular feature at each of the new locations.

- The November sales of Chunky Comics were huge: 436 copies of *Return of the Hunter,* and 424 copies of *The Lost Unicorn.* The production crew had to work afternoons, nights, and one full weekend to keep up with the demand.

- Near the end of November the Chunky Comics Group used some of its early profits to purchase an electric stapler and a good paper cutter to improve the speed and quality of their binding and trimming operations.

- In December the Chunky Comics rack offered three new minicomics, plus the original two. Two of the new titles were by Greg and Maura: *Creon: The Strong Survived* and *The Princess's Nightmare.* The third was a science-fiction comic written by Ted Kendall, drawn by Maura, and inked by Greg. It was called *The Trumpets of Mars.*

- In December, Maura began working on a new volume of minicomics about a girl detective computer genius named Haxy Spectrum. The first two issues were a huge hit, and those led to four more Haxy titles through the school year.

•Over the Christmas holidays Greg and Maura got some help from another sixth-grade friend and launched a simple Web site ChunkyComics.com—to tell the story of the business and also to collect e-mail addresses for an Internet version of the Chunky Comics Club.

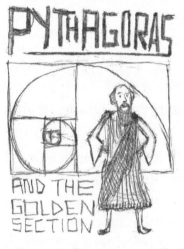

•In January, Chunky Comics also issued a nonfiction minicomic called *Pythagoras and the Golden Section*, written by Anthony Zenotopoulous, drawn by Maura Shaw, and inked by Greg Kenton. It was not one of the big sellers.

•By February, ChunkyComics.com was attracting more than 1,100 visitors each week.

•By April the Chunky Comics Club monthly e-mail newsletter was going out to more than 2,300 subscribers, and the first Internet orders were shipped. Sales of Chunky Comics at the school stores in town remained strong.

- By May comic book collectors on eBay were offering five to seven dollars for a copy of Chunky Comics, volume 1, number 1, in fine condition.

- In June, Mr. Z received approval to teach during the summer at the local community college. He had developed a course called "Turning Business Ideas into Realities."

- Through all the ups and downs of an incredibly busy school year, Maura and Greg both finished with grade averages between B plus and A minus—a tie, or almost a tie.

- Greg and Maura's partnership survived five major artistic disagreements, four heated arguments about money, two binding arbitration sessions with Mr. Z, and one awkward attempt at holding hands.

- In late June, Greg and his dad got a call from a woman who worked at one of the big book clubs. She wanted to know if Greg was interested in exploring the possibility of a national distribution deal for Chunky Comics. After consulting with the other key members of the group, Greg decided he was.

- Up on the stage during the awards assembly on the last day of school, Greg, Maura, and Mr. Z handed Mrs. Davenport a check for $1,421, a donation to the Ashworth Intemediate

School library on behalf of all the vendors who had sold their products through the school store.

•Nine hundred twenty-three dollars and thirty-eight cents of that total donation came directly from the Chunky Comics Group, and Greg Kenton could not believe how good it made him feel to give that money away.

THE END